By the same author

Brother, What Strange Place is This?
and other stories

Roof Whirl Away
and stories

Inappropriate Happiness

To the Boy
Poems

The Corner of Moon Street

stories

Tom Saunders

Reuben Books

First published in Great Britain, October 2016

Reuben Books, Dereham, NR20 5RB.

British Library Cataloguing in Publication Data.
A catalogue record for this book is available from the British Library.

Printed and bound by Azimuth Print.
Bookman Old Style 11/20

ISBN: 978-0-9562828-7-3

For my friends.

Contents

Contents

After Doris Day

After Doris Day came Brigitte Bardot. The shift in Atlas Jones's affections happened on a Sunday evening in July in the cool, dark nave of the Lido cinema in Ealing. This revolution in his world view – a narrow construct, admittedly, but one tight at the seams with emotion – was both abrupt and unconditional. The reek of cigarette smoke and overflowing ashtrays and the damp, swampy aroma of mouldering red plush seating would, from that moment on, be synonymous with sub-titles and sex, with a new and unruly kind of secret self, a secret self determined to shove its pointed ears and scaly snout into everything he did. Contemptuous of the freckled cheek and bright, anodyne smile of the now superseded Doris, it hungrily anticipated its first nibble from the apple of knowledge (not your French Golden Delicious even in metaphor, for this was back in the sixties, in the days of true taste and true temptation, when any shrewd serpent would certainly have made its bed in the sweet yellow flesh of the Cox's Orange Pippin).

Brigitte Bardot: high-priestess of the blatant, the impossible, the emphatically over the seas and far,

far away.

Post Doris Day, post And God Created Woman, Atlas Jones was a different sort of schoolboy. He saw with a frightening lucidity, sensitised suddenly to the dullness of the everyday, a dullness that appeared to lean in on him from all sides, one that would, in time, crush the juice, the fun, the surprise, from his life forever.

Defeat seemed unavoidable. How, when everyone else had apparently failed, could he hope to resist the old, the settled and the accepted? Sooner or later a numb suburban inertia would overtake him. He could already feel its power undermining his belief in all things loud and wild and vital. Rock'n'Roll for example: his music. Atlas still saw Cliff Richard with his flick-knife sneer, hair quiffed-up like a tidal wave in freeze-frame, as a rebel, but it was disconcerting when he spoke of his ambition to become "an all-round entertainer" in newspaper and magazine interviews. This Cliff wasn't the role-model Atlas needed. He needed someone to give him the courage to go his own way. What had happened to the moody rocker who once ordered his audience to get up and "Move it," who liked to boast that his girl gave him love in a barrel labelled "Dynamite"? The vision of a song-and-dance-man Cliff partnering a chill Brigitte understudy in some zillionth-rate production number and then crooning some daft ballad to her in the moonlight, was too grisly, too Hammer Horror to even joke about.

Elvis, too, having stilled his hips, cut his hair and gone into the army, had shown himself to be unworthy of consideration. Where was all that wriggling rebellion now? Was there any place for this God-and-Country momma's boy in the X certificate world of the irrepressible Brigitte? Brigitte who threw off her clothes with all the natural simplicity of a bird taking wing. Brigitte who knew no shame, who knew no code.

Perhaps to counter the suspicion that the unsurpassed B. B. had little substance outside of his hormonally-enriched imagination, he decided to write her a letter. In it, he reminded her of the vital part she'd been chosen to play in the fantasy life of the suburban adolescent. It was, he wrote, her duty to keep up the good work and take no notice of the gutter press and its prurient fixation with her breasts and backside. She should, he reassured her in closing, never be in any doubt as to the serious philosophical and cultural importance of her films.

In reply, he received an autographed pin-up picture of the star, a glossy 10" x 8" monochrome print. She had on a white bikini, staring out at him with a sly, big-toothed grin and pretending to catch a beach ball, her right leg kicked back and her long, blonde ponytail frozen in mid-dance. The signature, with its ripely-looped initials, wasn't handwritten but part of the photograph. She hadn't picked up a pen and, with him in mind, signed it personally. But he forgave her. He couldn't imagine the beautiful Brigitte sitting at a desk for countless hours scribbling her name for sad, self-conscious schoolboys with no chest hair to speak of such as himself. He wanted to see her as he always saw her, unfettered and running free.

The more Atlas had to do with the girls at school, the more he longed for his Brigitte. Where she optimised freedom and abandon at all times, they were loud and sharp-tongued together and shy on their own. Where she watched and said little, at a catlike remove and mysterious, they went over and over every relationship, every glance and word, worrying away at their feelings until nothing remained un-said. Where she'd absolutely no interest in what other people thought of her, they seemed to be more anxious about how their friends saw them than how they saw themselves. Where his Brigitte belonged to him alone, their attention was on the next lesson, the next dress, the next date, the next cut-price heartthrob with a dead-end job and a third-hand Ford Prefect.

Deirdre took him by surprise. She wasn't, until he noticed her, someone he'd normally have noticed. The truth was that when he saw her for the first time – actually saw her – she wasn't who he thought she was.

He was in Woolworth's stealing a red (not his pre-ferred colour, but the green ones were hard to reach without the risk of being caught) pencil-sharpener, when Deirdre, the pinch-lipped, exam-hound from the class above him in school, was revealed to him in all her blonde glory. Swinging casually around, stolen goods in his pocket, he almost tripped face first into her improbably-elevated bosom. The prox-imity of warm-scented skin was dizzying to the senses and his apology was a mumble in a language yet to be discovered. When he raised his eyes, he raised them to a dreamscape, a mademoiselle in a white broderie anglaise blouse and blue gingham skirt.

"Hello," she said without a trace of a French ac-cent.

It was hard for Atlas to breathe. His knees and hands shook. Her pale pink lipstick clung stickily to the pores of her mouth, which was pushed out as though someone had just stolen her last croissant, the top lip a bow, the bottom a cushion. Along the curve of her lower lashes she had drawn a thick line of eyebrow pencil. It finished in an exotic, flicked-up curlicue that continued on past the outer corner of the lid. Her yellow and gold hair was back-combed into a high plume that fell untamed to her shoulders, the front brushed down in a long fringe, her sooty eyes blinking as she peered at him from behind it like Bambi in the long grass.

"Have you seen," again the perfect English, "Pat Blount and Elaine Barrett?"

Atlas examined the question from all sides. It circled in his head, the words becoming more and more unreal. Why should Pat Blount be of any interest to Brigitte? It wasn't as if Pat Blount was of any interest to him. Pat Blount didn't know when she was well off. When he'd been in a good mood and taken pity on the poor sad girl at the last school social, walking across what seemed like miles and miles of empty floor to ask for a dance, she and the rest of her ugly sister gang had elbowed each other and laughed in his face.

Deirdre frowned and bent toward him, her perfume clouding the air once more. "Are you all right? I know you're a bit dim, but you could at least say something."

"Deir-dre?" His voice jumped up an octave, culminating in a squeak.

She shook her beautiful hair in annoyance. "Look, if you do see them, do me a favour and tell them I'll meet them outside Dorothy Perkins at half-past-three. You can," she moved her head to and fro in a futile attempt to maintain eye contact with Atlas, "do that for me, can't you?"

It took Atlas weeks to get over the embarrassment of this meeting. There really should, he complained to himself, be some sort of law against a schoolgirl in sensible shoes turning out to be a sex-kitten in

5

disguise. However, this didn't prevent him from seeing Deirdre in a soft new glow. Even without make-
up in her blazer and tie or marching dutifully across
the playground carrying an armful of books, even
when she sang all the correct words to the hymns in
assembly or sat in the window of the classroom opposite his own writing industriously, the memory of
how she'd looked that day remained with him. He
sought her out between classes, orchestrating "accidental" passing-bys on the corridors and smiling at
her with hideous sincerity in the hope she might
sanctify him with another of her insults. When the
bell rang at four-o'clock, he'd rush out to the school
gates and wait for her to come out with her friends,
trailing along after them at a discreet distance, a
pulsing of lust in the back of his throat. Worst of all,
he began to loiter around her house at night, looking up whenever a light came on in one of the bedrooms, wondering, his mouth dry, whether this was
where her evil arts worked their magic, where she
went about her transformation.

It was obvious: like stockings and suspenders,
like juveniles and delinquency, he and Deirdre were
fated to be with one another. But how was he to
trick her into accepting their mutual destiny and
see him as the hero he was determined to be?

"It can't be a blind date if she knows who you
are," said Brian Dunn. Brian had recently started
going with Elaine Barrett and a foursome seemed to
be the uncomplicated solution.

Atlas sighed. "It can if you don't tell her."

They were by the washbasins opposite the door to
the playground and Brian, comb in hand, was re-
establishing his image. Atlas felt only pity for him.
He had a Tony Curtis haircut, true, but beneath it
he had a Tony Hancock face. Belching to order was

Brian's solitary claim to celebrity as far as the boys at school were concerned. At the pictures, the leading lady and man would pucker up for the long passionate kiss and Dunn, his timing perfect, would throw back his head, mouth gaping like a hippo's, and give vent to a thunderous burp. It always got a laugh. Always.

"I don't know what you're frightened of. Why don't you just ask her yourself?"

"I'm not frightened."

Brian snorted. "Oh yeah, sounds like it."

"All right then," having to haggle was sordid, but Atlas had no choice, "I'll make it twenty."

"Twenty what?"

"Park Drive."

"You must be joking."

"Woodbine, then."

"Make it Senior Service and I'll think about it."

Atlas bought the cigarettes on the way home, buying some Gauloises for himself at the same time.

Atlas was astonished by how easily it was all arranged. It was clearly meant to be. He sat on the wall at the agreed rendezvous and practised smoking in the French style while he waited. Holding the cigarette in the corner of his mouth, he let it hang sulkily from his lower lip. This was the easy part. Keeping it there while speaking was where the expertise came in. "Deirdre," he gasped, "my beautiful Deirdre. It eez vary true zat I am not ze stranger you were expecting, but it eez also true zat I am not who you zink I am."

He was coughing and squinting, tears damp on his face, when a big Vauxhall pulled up at the kerb. Deirdre wound down the window and waved him over. "Come on, chop-chop, we're running late."

Atlas said nothing as he got into the car, sitting as

far away from her on the back seat as possible. He wiped his face and looked at his hands as they drove off. What was going on? Brian hadn't kept his side of the bargain, that was for sure. Not knowing what to say was bad enough, but not knowing where they were going or why they were going there and who or what they'd meet when they arrived, had him in a panic. They were not going to the Odeon in Southall as had been the plan, not in a hired car, not with Deirdre mostly zipped up in what he assumed, although he had no experience of evening wear, was some sort of cocktail dress.

Deirdre's nostrils twitched in his direction. "What's that awful smell?"

Atlas dogged out his cigarette in the ashtray in the car door, where it continued to smoulder in fitful spirals. "French tobacco," he managed to wheeze before another fit of grinding coughs shook him.

Deirdre stretched across and thumped him hard on the back. When he turned toward her with bulging eyeballs and a plum-coloured face, she began to giggle into her free hand, a rather unfeminine snuffling noise, a small animal rooting in the mud.

A resultant feeling of loss increased Atlas's annoyance. When Brigitte Bardot laughed it was a soft, husky, womanly sound. You wanted to hear it over and over again. "What's with the big motor?" he said. "Where's Brian and Elaine?" His throat felt raw and there was an embarrassingly whiny edge to his voice. Conscious that the driver was watching him in the rear-view mirror, he added, "I can't afford all this, you know." His fingers plucked at the Vauxhall's tatty interior as if it were the honeymoon suite at the Ritz. "I've only got a paper round."

Deirdre touched his wrist. "Okay, fine, keep calm. It's all settled, my dad's paying."

Atlas nodded as if vindicated. "Right."

"You're wearing jeans."

"You don't say." Atlas was tempted to point out that what was good enough for James Dean was good enough for him, but it was obvious what her reply would be.

"Never mind, I suppose it can't really be helped. It's all been at such short notice."

Atlas sighed in exasperation. "What has? And why should it have anything to do with my choice of trousers?"

"It's not your choice of trousers that's the problem. It's your non-choice of trousers. A nice pair of neatly-pressed slacks and I wouldn't be complaining."

Why men were prevailed upon to press their trousers until they were as sharp as knives was something Atlas had never been able to work out. A slight aerodynamic advantage didn't appear to be an adequate explanation. He decided this was perhaps not the occasion to argue the point. "Very sorry to embarrass you, I'm sure," he said.

"It's not me you're embarrassing, it's yourself."

Atlas shivered. It was like listening to his mother. "I'm still waiting to find out what you've done with Brian and Elaine."

"Love's young nightmare? They had better things to do. I loathe that boy anyway. He's revolting."

"No, he isn't." Atlas felt obliged to speak up for his own gender. "Not all the time. What about her? She looks like candy floss on a stick in that fluffy pink jumper of hers."

"She's a bit blowsy, that's all. She lacks taste."

Elaine lacked everything as far as Atlas was concerned.

Deirdre took hold of the straps of her dress and

settled herself back inside it with a shrug of the shoulders that reminded Atlas of a fighter pilot adjusting his parachute harness. "Not that you or any of the other boys at school have the first idea about fashion sense," she said. "This little number was designed in Paris. My mum bought it for the firm's dinner and dance last Christmas."

Atlas had no choice but to take a long appraising look at her. It was a mistake. The truth bubbled up in him, out of control. "The dress looks great," he said. "You look great. You could be a film star or something. Out of this world."

Deirdre yanked at the hem of her skirt and, with a shimmy of her behind, returned it to the safety zone below her knees. The deep green cloth of the dress was heavy and expensive, its surface as shiny as a ribbon on a box of chocolates.

Despite her reaction, Atlas could tell she wasn't in the least surprised by his confession. He retreated along the seat until he was as far from her as possible. "Brian told you my plan right away, didn't he? I bet he thinks he's so funny."

"I told you he was revolting."

"And you think it's hilarious, too, I suppose."

"Not at all. I find it rather sweet."

Sweet. Atlas shuddered and said nothing.

"You don't have to come with me."

Tonight, Deirdre's blonde sheaf of hair was gathered together with an ivory band. Her mouth looked soft and her dark-rimmed eyes shone.

"You know I do."

Evidently they were off to a party near Denham village. A birthday celebration for Chantal, one of the girls in Deirdre's ballet class. It was her eighteenth. "Don't you dare say a word about us still being at school," warned Deirdre, reaching across and jabbing a varnished fingernail into Atlas's chest. "This is a proper grown-up bash and we don't want them treating us like kids."

The house was detached and all on one level like something out of a Hollywood film. They could hear music and laughter as they got out of the car and every window in the place flamed with light. Chantal stood at the open front door greeting guests. She executed a little dance step on seeing Deirdre and they kissed and embraced in a cringe making way. Atlas had his sweaty hand shaken with a cool and somewhat reluctant grip. Chantal reminded Atlas of an ostrich with her huge, dark eyes and long neck. Her hair was a sleek, black cap, pulled back from her face and coiled so tightly on the top of her head her cheekbones looked like they might pop right through her skin.

"You are, aren't you? I can tell," she said to him, turning him toward the light and scanning his features. "You have the same nose."

Atlas blinked at her. "Am I? Do I?"

Deirdre took his arm with a quick panicky smile. "Of course he is," she said. "Pay no attention to him, he just likes to tease. Chantal, this is my younger brother, Atlas. Atlas, this is Chantal. Say happy birthday, Atlas."

Atlas showed his teeth and did as he was told.

"Hello, I'm Leo." A large, chimp-eared young man in a navy blue blazer and grey flannels slithered out from behind Chantal. He offered his hand to Deirdre and peered into the ripe divide of her cleavage.

Chantal rolled her eyes and drew him back by the arm. "That's Leo as in Leo my fiancé. Or ex-fiancé if he doesn't behave himself."

Further introductions were made. Leo crushed Atlas's fingers while still staring at Deirdre. "Unusual name your brother has," he said.

Deirdre, bless her, did her best to look puzzled. "Is it?"

He paused for effect, excruciatingly pleased with himself. Oil glistened in his impeccably-parted hair. His large, smooth jaw glowed pink above the custard-coloured cravat at his throat. "One can only assume," he said in a rush when Deirdre took Atlas's hand and attempted to walk by, "that your father was a travelling salesman of some kind." He nudged Chantal and honked like a goose. "Atlas. Travelling salesman. Get it?"

Atlas would have liked to have looked down on Leo witheringly, but without a stepladder this was impossible. "I'm glad you find it amusing," he said.

"I do, old chum, I do."

Deirdre came to the rescue. "I think it's a very distinguished name. Atlas was a king. A man strong enough to support the entire globe on his shoulders."

"Ha, good one," Leo said, cuffing Atlas on the back with a friendly paw and all but knocking him off his feet. "Better start eating up all your greens then, eh."

Chantal and Leo took them inside. People were dancing in the large living room. The music was Latin American and awful.

The hosts of the party lay in wait.

Chantal's mum, Arabella, was short and plump with a wispy corona of tangerine hair. She smiled benignly at Atlas. "We're enchanted to have such a handsome young man here, aren't we, Dermot?"

Dermot was tall and skinny like his daughter. Together with Leo and several other men at the party he wore a blazer, flannels and a cravat. He jabbed the stem of his pipe in the direction of Atlas's chest and spoke to the room as if he were addressing a meeting. "Have to smarten himself up considerably if he's to make anything of himself, though."

Arabella frowned at her husband and shook her head. She took Atlas in a protective arm-lock and swept him off toward the open sliding doors to the garden in a cloud of perfume. "Silly man, silly man," she muttered to herself. "Let's get you a drink."

Atlas looked over his shoulder and saw a disloyal and unconcerned Deirdre moving off with Chantal and Leo. He was on his own.

The bar was on the lawn near the swimming pool. It was made up of long trestle tables and there was a blue and white striped awning above it.

"What would you like, Atlas, dear?" Arabella had on a silver dress cut from some sort of thick twinkling material. When she turned, the bodice, a rigid structure similar to a pair of conical gun-turrets, remained pointing straight ahead.

Atlas was all set to choose. He had tasted nothing stronger than the occasional sip of his father's pale ale at Christmas. A regimental display of bottles crowded the table top before him, bottles of every measure, shape and tint. A flunky with a thin David Niven moustache stood waiting behind the bar. His short white coat made Atlas want to order two ice-cream cornets and a raspberry split.

"How about," Arabella squeezed his arm, "some orange crush or would you prefer lemonade?"

Silently aggrieved, Atlas settled on a glass of Coke. It was just possible someone would think there was a shot of rum in it.

Arabella pinched his cheek and laughed as he flinched away. "Later on, Dermot will put some of Chantal's Pat Boone records on the radiogram and you youngsters will have a chance to jive or whatever it is they call it these days."

Atlas rubbed his face as she jiggled off to greet the newest arrivals at the party. "I'm not who you think I am," he called after her in a hurt voice.

The garden and terrace were dotted with couples and small groups of people talking and drinking. Atlas drifted over to the swimming pool and stood looking into it. It wasn't big by Californian standards, but the water was a vivid Technicolor blue and agreeably unreal. Along with the smell of chlorine there was a faint whiff of hot lilo and wet towel.

Atlas moved amongst the groups. No-one would look at him. Bored, he returned to the living room ... or was it the lounge? It was impossible to tell without the benefit of one of the new sociological surveys. There was a zebra skin on the wall above the stone fireplace, which was so wide it could have doubled as a small cave. Atlas sipped his Coke in what he hoped was an adult fashion and avoided the dancers. He decided the furniture must be contemporary. He'd heard the style identified as that on TV. There were half a dozen armchairs and three sofas with spindly black legs and thin, square cushions covered with large, colourful motifs.

He ran into Deirdre by the door to the kitchen. She had a full glass of champagne in her hand. "Leo brought it along for Chantal's birthday," she said gulping a mouthful. "He nearly shot one of the caterers with the cork." When Atlas tried to go with her, she pushed him away. "Don't tag around after me like a little dog. Enjoy the party." Holding her glass above her head, she circulated the room, talking and laughing in a phoney way and waving her arms about in an exaggerated fashion.

Atlas ventured further into the house. He knew he could say he was in search of the lavatory if anyone

14

asked him where was going.

In the largest of the bedrooms there was a vast double-bed with green silk sheets. The carpet was a tone or two darker. Several white fluffy rugs lay on it like patches of unthawed snow on a lawn. A long fitted wardrobe with mirrored doors faced the bed. When Atlas walked toward it, his twin came to meet him, a shifty-eyed scoundrel if there ever was one. A nosy scoundrel, too. There were a dozen or so suits in Dermot's side of the wardrobe and two more blazers. Arabella had three fur coats hanging in a line, a black one, a brown one and a silvery grey one. They were zipped up in clear protective bags and they made Atlas think of bears wearing plastic macs.

Chantal's bedroom was across the hall. A china ballerina in a pink tutu stood next to the make-up bag on the dressing table. She was poised on the point of one shoe, her other leg stretched out behind her like the tail of a helicopter. The room was considerably smaller and cosier than Dermot and Arabella's and it smelt faintly of cheesy footwear and very strongly of perfume and talcum powder. A pair of red satin ballet shoes dangled by their ribbons from a brass picture hook above the bed. Atlas took a book at random from the shelves under the window. It was a novel about a plucky young girl living on a hill farm. Her best friend was her horse.

Back at the party all the blazers and cravats were striking manly poses and smoking furiously. The only other time Atlas could remember seeing so many men puffing on pipes was in a World War II film about the Battle of Britain.

Alcohol had made the dancing more approximate. Big beefy chaps raised on rowing and rugby grappled moistly with their partners.

Atlas stood watching in disbelief. He didn't see

Arabella until it was too late. She took him by the hand and told him he must dance with Chantal and give Leo a rest. He did his best to say no, but his protest was stalled by Chantal coming by and whirling him off into the music and sweat. Every time he trod on her foot, she kicked him and smiled pleasantly. An angry football game would have been less painful.

He was only set free when Perry Como dropped down from the auto-changer. When it came to the smoochy stuff, Chantal wanted her Leo and Leo wanted his Chantal.

There was a buffet on the far side of the room. Atlas joined the queue of hungry dancers helping themselves. He took a paper plate and loaded it up with potato salad and cubes of Cheddar and cocktail sausages impaled on sticks and found a quiet corner where he could eat and feel abandoned. He'd no genuine appetite, but he set about cramming the food down with a resentful deliberation. His mood wasn't improved when Deirdre slow-danced past snuggled up between the outrageous biceps of a lanky charmer with a ginger crew-cut and a jaw the size of a fire-bucket.

Around midnight, the music stopped in the middle of a record. There was a burble of surprise then expectancy amongst the party-goers. Dermot was about to give a speech. Arabella started to shepherd people out on to the lawn, organising them into a semi-circle facing the terrace. When Dermot appeared, he'd changed into a chunky woollen cardigan with a belt and a folded-over collar, decorated with a frieze of reindeer in silhouette. Bracing himself with a long, meditative draw on his pipe, he held up a palm to still the applause that Arabella, clapping mightily and glaring at those around her, only then began to lead.

Dermot clutched the collar of his cardigan with his free hand and cleared his throat. "Thank you," he said. "Thank you."

The applause petered out raggedly.

"It's getting late so I won't bore you with a lot of words. As you're all well aware this party is to celebrate the eighteenth birthday of our darling daughter, Chantal." He smiled at Chantal and Arabella. They both looked at him with melting affection. "What you also no doubt know, is that she is now engaged to Leo Tutt, a good friend of yours and," he smiled again, "I hope in the future, in his role as a hard-working, responsible husband, a good friend of mine."

All heads turned to a deeply discomfited Leo. He and Chantal were standing with their arms around each other's waists. She moved closer and gazed up at him, a wet glint in her eyes. "Don't you fret, sir," he said, "I'll do my duty. Although," he gave Chantal a squeeze that almost lifted her off her feet, "I'm sure your daughter is more than capable of looking after herself."

Atlas wanted to blow a raspberry so badly his lips ached. If the way Leo had thrust his nose into Deirdre's bosom earlier was any indication of his future fidelity, it would be quicker to geld the bugger right now with a broken bottle and have done with it.

Dermot sucked on his pipe and nodded. "That, I must say, has been our experience, hasn't it, darling?" Arabella, back from organising the waiters who had now finished giving out the champagne, crossed to her husband's side and put her head on his chest.

"So," Dermot raised his glass, "I'd like to propose

17

a toast to our very own birthday girl. Happy birthday, Chantal, my sweet."

Atlas mumbled along with the rest of the partygoers before gulping down the glass of champagne he'd successfully grabbed from one of the passing trays. The wine tasted like his mother's Babycham and made his nose itch. It was pleasant but no more than that – a bit of a disappointment, in fact.

Now the celebratory formalities were over, people began to wander off into the house and toward the bar, their voices swelling in volume. Dermot, Arabella and Chantal had fallen into a three-way clinch in the meantime, huddling together the way children do when they have a secret to share. As Atlas trailed after a tray of drinks with his empty glass, he drew closer to them. Dermot's head bobbed up and down and, beginning with an explosive whimper, he began to cry in long, jarring sobs. Arabella and Chantal held on to Dermot tightly as their own tears started to flow as they attempted to console him. After swallowing noisily and with difficulty, he said, "I'm sorry, I can't help thinking about your mother and I losing you. You're so grown-up, now . . . so grown-up."

Chantal sniffed a moist sniff. "Oh don't, daddy. Don't say that. You know how much I love you and mummy. Don't."

Deirdre was sitting on the driveway propped up against the side of the Vauxhall when Atlas found her. "Oh there you are," she said. She tried to slap him on the wrist as if he had been naughty and missed. "Another few minutes and we'd have given up. The driver's just gone for one last look for you."

Atlas stood over her with his hands on his hips. "That's clever because I've been searching everywhere for you."

"You have?"

"It's late."

"'Better get on home'," Deirdre sang in reply.

"What about your mum and dad?"

"What about them?"

"What will they say?"

A glassy clink announced the return of the driver. The necks of two beer bottles protruded from his jacket pocket and there was a cocktail stick between his teeth. He grunted amiably at Atlas and they both crouched to lift Deirdre on to her feet and into the car.

The driver was in a relaxed mood. As the Vauxhall swung with a squealing of tyres out of the gates at the end of the driveway, a limp and giggling Deirdre slid along the bench seat toward Atlas. Hanging on to his thigh for support, she squinted up at him, her eyes not quite focusing. "What's up with you?" she said. "Why are you so angry? I'm giving you a lift, aren't I?"

"You're paralytic," Atlas said, staring down at her hand.

Deirdre let go of him and wriggled from side to side in an endeavour to sit upright. When the car rounded a bend in the opposite direction, she slide away as abruptly as she'd arrived, coming to a stop at the far end of the seat with a rustle and a bump.

"Are you all right?" Atlas asked.

Deirdre sighed. "Simply fantastic. What a perfect, perfect party. Didn't you think so, Atlas? Wasn't it utterly and truly wonderful?"

"Utterly." Atlas succeeded in empowering the word with a measure of irony that surprised even him.

"Cornelius's father is going to buy him a Jaguar for his twenty-first. A sports car."

"Cornelius?" Atlas said, laughing. "Who's he? Not the big red-faced bloke with the bristly haircut?"

Deirdre's pout was audible. "I like his hair. It's clean and neat. He let me feel it and it tickles."

"I think he fancies himself."

"Not half as much as you would if you were at university studying to be a lawyer. This winter he's off on a skiing holiday. He's already been away on a trip to France this year."

Atlas grunted in disgust. "France, what would a bloke like him know about France."

"I see," Deirdre said, her eyes glinting in the darkness, "you've been there, have you?"

"It's not a question of the place itself. It's a feeling."

"You don't know what you're talking about."

Atlas shook his head angrily and turned to look out the window. "What's the point. You wouldn't understand."

"There's nothing to understand, if you ask me."

Atlas shrugged and remained silent.

Deirdre kicked off her shoes, tucked her legs under her on the seat and rested her cheek against the window, her profile softly-lit, her lips parted. When she spoke it wasn't so much to Atlas as to herself. "One day I'd love to be able to throw fantastic parties like Chantal and her parents. It must be incredible to live in a beautiful modern house with a swimming pool and everything."

"With old Cornelius?"

"I could do worse."

"You could do better."

"When I get married I know exactly how it's going to be."

Atlas yawned noisily.

"I'm going to have pageboys in red satin suits with lace collars and bridesmaids in baby pink and white and my dress will be layers of satin and tulle, crisp as icing on a cake . . ."

Atlas groaned.

" . . . and the men will be wearing morning dress, Ascot ties, grey tail-coats and top hats . . ."

Atlas put his hands over his ears. His only suit (and it didn't fit him any more) had been bought for his cousin's wedding, an awkward anti-climatic affair that had taken place in a featureless chamber off a featureless corridor in the featureless building that was the Uxbridge Registry Office.

" . . . and my husband," there was obstinacy and malice in her voice now, she wasn't going to let anyone spoil what was close to her and make her think less of herself, "will be someone with a career, a profession and I'll write for one of the glossy fashion magazines – no, better than that, I'll be an editor . . ."

Atlas didn't know what he wanted to do when he left school. None of the jobs available to him, that was certain.

" . . . and we'll have a good car, not just a black box with four wheels and four seats . . . and we'll go travelling on the Continent in the summer for our holidays . . . and we'll have three children, two girls and a boy . . ."

"You'll be telling me their names next."

Deirdre rounded on him, her voice angry. "So what is it you want out of life, then, eh?"

"Not any of that."

"What, then?"

"Just not that," Atlas said with a scowl.

Deirdre laughed a bitter laugh. "You don't know, do you? You haven't got a clue."

Earlier that evening, all Atlas wanted out of life would have involved Deirdre on a double bed wearing nothing but a pair of stockings and some lacy black drawers. Now he wasn't so sure.

"Do you want to live in a slum?"

"No, of course not."

"What about a car? You'd like a car, wouldn't you?"

"I wouldn't mind."

"A nice one?"

"I suppose so."

Deirdre folded her arms. "So you want all the things I want, but you're just not honest enough to admit it to yourself."

Atlas knew this was untrue. Proving it to her and to himself would be another thing, so he kept quiet.

After a while, Deirdre's breathing became slow and regular and she began to snore, at first rather delicately, then, after a sequence of prefatory snorts, like a pneumatic road drill. At the next corner she slid, limp as yesterday's lettuce, back along the seat and came to rest with her head on Atlas's shoulder.

They stayed like this, together but not together, touching but not touching, for the remainder of the journey. The end of Atlas's street came and went without him saying anything to the driver. He couldn't just get out and leave her, could he?

When the Vauxhall pulled up outside Deirdre's house, Atlas gently disentangled himself. "Deirdre," he whispered, supporting her shoulder and giving it a shake. "Deirdre, we're here."

She opened her eyes slowly and stretched. "Oh, right." For a second it was as though she wasn't certain who he was. "Have you paid the driver?"

Atlas sighed. "I can't. You told me your dad's going to pay."

"Y-es," Deirdre said, hesitating fleetingly before regaining her usual self-confidence. "Well he is. Of course he is. I remember now."

"The house looks dark."

She dipped her head and looked out. "So it does. Well," the smile on her face in the light of the street-lamp was inscrutable, "I really can't say I'm surprised."

"You can't?"

"No." She yawned. "Anyway, I have enough to deal with it."

They got out of the car. Atlas watched as Deirdre counted pound notes into the driver's palm from a thick wad of cash produced from her handbag.

"Your parents must trust you," Atlas said as the Vauxhall drove off. "There's no way my parents would let me walk around with that sort of money even if we had it."

Deirdre smiled her strange indecipherable smile again. "Nor would mine if they knew."

Atlas laughed nervously. "Yeah, right."

"Don't stare at me like that, it's the truth."

"They don't know you've got it?"

"No."

"So where's it come from?"

"Does it matter?"

"Of course it bloody-well does."

"Only to you."

"And not your parents?"

"If you must know I borrowed it."

"Borrowed?" Atlas took a moment before he understood. "You stole it?" His voice echoed along the street.

Deirdre covered his lips with her fingers. "Shush, big mouth. No, I borrowed it. No need to wet yourself. It's no concern of yours."

"You're not wrong there."

"No, I'm not. You should know that by now."

Atlas swore quietly. "I should have known straight away there was something weird about this whole set-up. Driving up to me in a hired car. Why did you even bother with me, that's what I want to know?"

"I had to have an escort. A girl can't go to a party without an escort. It's not done."

"I'm the one who's been done. I just wanted to go to the pictures."

"I don't see what you're making such a fuss about," Deirdre said with a shake of her head. "I'll pay it back. I'm going to start a Saturday job and save up."

"Bloody hell."

"There's no need to worry. Honestly."

Atlas tried to look her in the eye, but she kept turning away from him. "What else is going on? Your parents do know about the party, I hope."

"Not exactly."

"Great. That means no."

"Sort of. They know about it, but they said I couldn't go."

"You must be crazy to think you could sneak off and come back this late without being caught. Does your mum know you're wearing her dress?"

"What do you think?"

Atlas held his hands up in exasperation. "No wonder there's no-one in. Your parents are probably down at the local cop shop right this minute. With the money gone and you not home they'll think you've run off who knows where."

Deirdre frowned. "I don't see how. They won't be back until tomorrow night."

"What?" Atlas said, shaking his head as if to clear it.

"They're not here."

"Not here?"

"No."

Atlas took Deirdre by the arms. "Look, will you

24

please tell me what exactly is going on?"

The truth was that Deirdre's mum and dad had needed to take some things down to their caravan on the south coast and left her in the charge of her older brother. And he, tantalised by the anticipation of a night of love and lust with his girlfriend, had all but propelled Deirdre out of the door when Elaine came calling. He had given Deirdre the key and told her to let herself in and go straight to bed when she got back. Deirdre had smuggled the dress out in a carrier bag and changed at Elaine's.

"And the money? Where did you get that?"

"I took it from the cashbox mum uses for her accounts."

"They'll kill you."

Deirdre shrugged. "She told me it was for emergencies."

"That's never going to work."

Deirdre's laughter was so sudden it caught in her throat and made her cough. "No, I don't suppose it will. But it'll blow over eventually. It always has in the past."

Atlas could only stare silently at her lovely face, at her disobedient schoolgirl grin. What a fool she had made of him. What a fool he had made of himself. How could he ever have thought she might be the one he was looking for? His Brigitte. His incomparable Brigitte.

"Aren't you going to give me a kiss?"

Atlas hesitated.

"There's no need to be frightened."

"I am not frightened," said Atlas, frowning at her.

It was a good kiss, but not a great one. Atlas would never be able to explain why he chose to slide his hand over her breast. Enclosing it in his palm, he squeezed it speculatively like someone assessing a piece of fruit in a greengrocer's shop. The material of her dress had a cool, slippery feel.

A solitary squeeze was all he got. Deirdre twisted away from him and punched him on the arm. "The trouble with you, Atlas," she said, "is that you've got a one track mind."

Later, Atlas would wish he had found the words at that moment to tell her just what a magnificent place this one track could lead to. A place where the biggest and warmest sun shone all day long, where the cool, clear night sky always glittered with stars.

Deirdre had a good deal more she had to say about Atlas. "Now, I don't want you to get upset, but you must realise that I can't possibly go out with you again. I'm not saying I don't like you a lot. Or that, in your own odd way, you're not a very nice boy." She looked into his eyes soulfully, her sympathy an arrow through his proud heart. "It's just that to be perfectly honest, I think you've got a certain amount of growing up to do."

There was a pause. Atlas, who was now staring hard at his shoes and not about to look up, assumed she was waiting for him to answer.

"All right?" she prompted.

He nodded.

"No hard feelings?"

~~~

After Brigitte Bardot came Sophia Loren. Light giving way to dark. Sophia, Atlas's Sophia, was a woman not a girl. In her films she was an unconquerable force. In Two Women, she played a mother who was prepared to surrender herself for her child. Brigitte, for all her freedom, seemed spoilt by comparison. And Sophia was constant. Her favour might be difficult to win, but once it was bestowed it was twice as difficult to lose. She possessed a peasant loyalty that was not easily swayed. If she came to see you as one of her own she would be generous with both her affection and her anger and yet never let you go.

Atlas was in awe of her physical magnificence, her strong, bountiful figure evoking a world of simplicity and plenty, where olive trees were blown by Mediterranean winds, where ordinary people like himself, raised on a diet of pasta and Chianti, were joyous and uninhibited. Not that there wasn't an ambiguity to her beauty. She was good-humoured and laughed loud and often, but her dark gypsy face had a suggestion of cruelty in repose, eyebrows curved like scimitar blades, nose long and straight and keenly outlined, lips wide and full, close to harsh in their perfection – a warning perhaps that she should never be taken for granted.

Long after he had become himself, a husband and a father and happily so, Atlas thought he glimpsed Sophia on Bond Street in London. She was wearing a grey fur hat and a grey fur coat and cuddling a tiny dog with the face of a gargoyle. Later, he read an article in the newspaper claiming she was in Los Angeles making a film with some lucky leading man or other at the time, so perhaps it was, as with Deirdre all those years before, just another case of mistaken identity. Nevertheless, the woman who was not Sophia Loren did smile at him as they passed and he carried this smile around with him like a Get Out of Jail Free card for the rest of the day.

Anthropology

Deejay Hanno Boshannon, spiralling in the ratings and about to be fired, lost the will to spin during the early morning weather report, the forecast sunny with a high pollen count. A bottle of vodka, two smashed CD players, a striptease and a bowel movement later, the show's producer finally reclaimed the studio for the radio station by anaesthetising the squatting Boshannon with a blow from a stale baguette one of the engineers had left behind in the control room.

Boshannon, following several weeks in a calm, white clinic in the suburbs and bereft of radio work and professional pride, met Thea while moonlighting for an office cleaning company. He was emptying wastepaper baskets in the anthropology department of Imperial College and she was backside uppermost on the floor of her office, the beads of a broken fertility amulet scattered underfoot. She turned to appraise him as he got down on his knees to help and asked if he ever waxed his chest hair. He attempted a denial, but she wasn't listening.

Later, in bed, Kensington love rites complete, he listened to her with his mouth shut and his demeanour open, he the supplicant, she the shaman.

"You're an ugly man," she said, "and to the non-scientific mind looks are everything. People in general pay a great deal of attention to the superficial and it's easy to understand why. The deeper problems of the world are unpleasant and they never go away. Much better to focus on your toes, which are particularly unattractive. If and when they come up with a cosmetic fix I'd advise you to invest in it."

Thea paused for a nod from Boshannon.

"To tell you the truth, you seem rather depressed to me," she continued. "A gold star for effort and bless you for the thought, but I don't think oral sex is supposed to be quite so desperate. You need to bolster your sense of worth. It doesn't matter how little substance there is to the reality. Self-belief is vital. It's much better to believe you're more beautiful and more intelligent than everyone else than it is to be more beautiful and more intelligent than everyone else."

The affair lasted three months. It ended when Boshannon found a job on a small radio station on the Isle of Wight.

He interrupted Thea for the first time on their last evening together. "My turn now, angel," he said. "I've learnt a lot from you since we got it on," he told her, "and, apart from my new fear of showing my toes in public, every bit of it has rung a bell."

"I'm glad," Thea said with a smile that avoided any lack of self-satisfaction.

Boshannon held up his hand and shook his head. He was working. The magic had returned. There was a show to be done and the buttons and faders of communication felt comfortable under his fingertips.

"For most of my life," he continued, "I've shot my mouth off in an industry that's almost entirely without significance or merit. Because of you, I'm now aware of what a gift this has been and how crazy I was to imagine otherwise. You, on the other hand, are a babe and seven-eighths and yet you're cool about busting the clock studying and cataloguing information that's of little interest to any fucker, least of all the objects of your study. And despite knowing this you still walk the walk. Such brass balls and confidence are really something special."

"Yes, well, I'm not sure . . ." Thea began hesitantly and then faltered.

Boshannon pulled on his boxers and stood up and looked at himself in the mirror by the bed. "Because of this," he said with a yawn, "I plan to dedicate a song to you and your regal behind each morning for as long as I'm on the air and commercial. A bad song, no doubt, and not of my choosing, but listening to you I've come to realise that to care too much, or even slightly, would be to care needlessly and without hope."

Economics

It is what will become an ordinary day. Bellamy
sits down on a bench in the high street to read
his newspaper. He has too much time to fill but
not enough time, he discovers as he turns the
pages, to make sense of all the bad things going on
in the world.

He is disturbed by the muttering of a man hunch-
ing secretively over the screen of a nearby cash dispenser. The muttering grows louder until, with a
grunt of anger, the man kicks the wall and slaps his
palm down on the keyboard. "Consult my bank?" he
says, his voice climbing in pitch, angry adult becoming hurt child. "This *is* my bank."

He is a very tall man. The weather is hot, but he is
wearing a dark, wide-shouldered suit and a trilby
hat. He looks like a crook in an old British B picture, a gang boss with a dubious American accent,
feet up on the desk in the backroom of some im-
probably ritzy night-club in Soho.

The machine fails to respond and he lifts his eyes
to the sky. "I do have cash in my account," he says,

bending down to speak into the machine and enunciating with care, perhaps convinced there is someone small, deaf and incompetent within. "I *know* I have cash in my account." Keeping his head lowered, he listens for a moment, hat crushed against the top of the metal hatchway, and then steps back and rattles a few buttons, sighing an afflicted sigh as he does so. When he ducks down a second time the trilby falls off and the next person in line – a red-haired woman wearing a peasant blouse, long skirt and sandals – picks it up nervously and holds it against her chest like a soldier at a funeral.

The man's right hand balls into a fist. "You've made a mistake. Give me my money. I *want* my money. You *have* to give me my money. If you don't I'm going to stay right where I am until you do." There is a tremor in his voice, the tremor of a decent individual radicalised by injustice.

The resolution in his tone prompts several people at the end of the queue – which has continued to expand conga fashion, the optimism of the British public irrepressible – to walk way. With a penguin flap of their arms they move off to try elsewhere. Those electing to remain share their fortitude with a shrug and a smile and shift uneasily from one foot to the other, sensing, perhaps, that their safe, orderly universe is bending out of shape.

Bellamy is equally uneasy. Intervention is a reflex with him. Bystanding has never been his style. The effort it takes for him to sit and watch and do nothing causes his ribs to ache. He sees a situation and situations scare and attract him, situations and dealing with them successfully were what his life before retirement had been about. Someone here needed to step in and take charge, take responsibility. A few words of reason, a brotherly guiding hand, would almost certainly be enough. The man deserved this at least. It is a lonely feeling to believe you are the only person prepared to stand firm against the chaos. And it is difficult to stay locked in with your anger when the light of an open door beckons.

The one strategy that will not work, Bellamy knows, is to try and tell the man he is being stupid. Strange indeed that you can understand the idiocy of your own actions with the objectivity of a third party and still not be able to stop: "I am making a fool of myself, but they made me do it. They made me. They."

"They" had made Bellamy retire. He lifts his newspaper, takes refuge inside its pages. Not this time, he tells himself, it is not going to be me this time. All of that is in the past. But it is impossible. He cannot read for listening. First there is one voice from the body of the queue, then two, then a choir in querulous counterpoint. Men threaten deep and women entreat high. The traffic noise is a bass rumble to be shouted above.

Bellamy shuts the paper with a puff of exasperation. When he stands up to leave, the movement draws the eyes of several of the people gathered on the pavement, their faces seeking somebody to trust like children in need of a grown-up. This is not fair, said their expressions. It should not be allowed. We are not asking too much. Why us?

And yes, the man at the cash dispenser is still waiting for his money, arms braced on the keyboard, elbows spread to make his shoulders bigger and hinder any interruption, everything else blocked out and excluded. Which, apart from enraging the people behind him even further, only makes it easier for the two young men who eventually step from the rear of the queue and seize him by the arms and drag him backwards. After a further struggle, a tango for three, he is thrown at a stagger to the floor.

Bellamy pauses at the corner and glances back. The line at the cash-point has reformed and is now shuffling forward at a pace that seems almost spiteful. Ignored now, the man gets to his feet slowly and limps off, right hand patting dust from the arse of his trousers. When, with a call and a wave, the woman in the peasant blouse pursues him and attempts to put his hat back on his head, he flinches away from her causing it to land aslant over one ear.

Goodbye Old Friend

Steve and I grew up on the same street, on the same Council estate on the western fringe of London. We went to the same schools and we were on nodding terms throughout our childhoods. We became real friends in our late teens, when we found ourselves in the same class at Technical College. We were both engineering apprentices. I worked for a firm a few miles away and Steve worked for one in our local town. As apprentices we were sent to be schooled one day a week. Living so near to one another it was inevitable we would travel to and from college together. From then on we were great friends.

He was with me when I met Jennifer. He and I were out for a drink one Friday night and we happened to go to the Everyman Liberation Club, a socialist/anarchist group of friends who got together for beer, absurdity and affable mayhem in a back room at the Royal Oak pub. When we arrived, Jennifer was talking to a girl I knew called Dawn. Steve and I joined in with the conversation. It was a meeting that turned out to be the most important meeting of my life.

Jennifer became Steve's friend, too. She, like me, found him easy company and the three of us spent a lot of time together. When Jennifer and I got married, Steve was my best man.

He spent Christmas at our house over the next few years. Then the offer of a much better job took him away to the other side of the country, where he later met and married Hazel, a person very much like Jennifer. They came and stayed with us when we were living in Torquay, Devon. Hazel was pregnant with Daisy, their first child, at the time. They went on to have another daughter named Tilly. Both lovely children. Our families spent as much time together as we could despite living quite some way apart. We shared holidays in Cornwall and Wales and when we moved out from London they would regularly come for weekends with us and we would go to them.

Steve was always a very stylish character and somewhat vain about his appearance. He was a man with an idea of himself. Unlike me, he always knew how to dress. Women were often attracted to him. At some point, he got involved with another woman and his marriage to Hazel ended. We liked Hazel (and still do) and we were very upset to see them split. Steve was always (apart from near the end) an almost unfathomable man and I could never get the details of the affair out of him or what happened in the relationship subsequently. He just would not talk about his feelings. His love life after the divorce remained a vague and awkward subject. But if he didn't want to talk about it, that was fine by me.

After the split with Hazel we gradually saw less and less of Steve. Months, sometimes years, went by without a visit or a phone-call from him. One Christmas he arrived without warning, stayed a few days and then drifted off again, disappearing back into his other existence. There were newer, younger friends he told us about and we assumed he was out with them enjoying a single life. Then, about eighteen months ago, he turned up looking ill and very down and told us that he had been diagnosed with emphysema. We were shocked to see the condition he was in and it was a very emotional visit. Not being able to do anything made it worse. It seems Steve had been on his own a lot of the time, smoking a great deal and not eating properly and losing weight (which, as a very slim man, he could not afford to lose) and generally not looking after himself. Because, as with us, he had been saying nothing while drifting in and out of the lives of Hazel and Daisy and Tilly and all his other friends, no-one knew what was going on with him. The saddest thing was that he opened up to me like never before on his last couple of visits. "I made a big, big mistake," he told me on both occasions. He knew at last, as we all did, that he would never have got sick if he had stayed in his marriage. Hazel would have looked after him.

All too soon, Steve's lungs began to fail completely.

I have many, many happy memories of Steve. There were innumerable good times. It wasn't a sad life. Perhaps my favourite recollection as I write this is of a Christmas we spent with Steve and Hazel. We were on our way back from a party at one of their friend's houses, a little bit drunk and happier, perhaps, than we realised at the time. The party, old-fashioned and good-humoured, with most of Steve and Hazel's neighbours, both old and young, sitting neatly on chairs arranged against the walls of the small front room, amused then charmed us. When we left, we found it had been snowing heavily and the snow was smooth and thick on the ground. It was frosty with a sharpness in the air and the sky was clear and there were stars beyond stars shining down on us. We were all in a wonderful mood. We liked each other and ourselves and everyone else in the world. Steve and I, the boys we never stopped being, were running around and snowballing and I managed to get one over on him and he tumbled backwards into a snow drift. He was laughing as he fell and he landed with his arms spread wide. Instead of getting up, he lay where he was in the snow, looking up at the sky and laughing the kind of nothing left out, soul-deep, up from the shoes kind of laugh that defies everything.

I can hear it right now.

In an Old Country

It was a white winter's day, the smoky grey sky holding back the sun. Icicles dripped from the branches of the trees that overhung the drive. Mist dissolved the dark bulk of the shrubs edging the lawns. There was a furring of haw frost on the grass and the withered leaves of the flowers in the ornamental urns on either side of the steps up to the house.

I was tired, faded with the journey, soft at the edges. A moment this unlikely could only feel imaginary. Life sometimes changes so fast it leaves you spinning in its slipstream. I was present yet notional. Only belief could have made me real.

The bell-pull was cold in a hand not quite my own. Its jangle jolted me back into real time and I heard birdsong, smelt the damp of the stonework.

"Yes?" An elderly woman peered around the door at me as if alarmed by the light, the question a challenge. The lenses of her glasses glinted as she looked me up and down, the vagueness in her brown eyes enlarged.

~~~

My room was above the roofline at the top of the house. It was small and stuffy, dust in the air. The radiator clicked as it worked up a sweat. There was a single dormer window with a view of tree-tops, outbuildings. The servants had once lived here, I had been told. Slept not lived, I thought to myself. I had a bed, a chair, a bookcase. I was to make myself at home. I turned slowly in a circle, dropped my bag.

My evening meal, a fancy French takeaway with food warmers and covered plates, had arrived mysteriously in the small kitchen along the landing from my room. It was eaten with my mentor, the personal assistant, a Mrs Anslem, Kara. I was her charge, claimed with a smile from the empty hallway soon after my arrival, alerted, I assumed, by the old lady.

Kara was businesslike in expensive black. I felt nugatory in my cheap blues and greys. She was a tall, attractive, tensely gaunt woman with an improbable tan. Leathery lines drew together the skin around her eyes and the corners of her mouth. Her too black, dyed hair was worn short, cut high on her neck, the sides angled, geometrically precise.

"I'd normally do the word processing on the novel," she explained, pouring me a glass of wine, "but I'm involved with the autobiography. It's taking time to fact-check and get permissions and there's pressure from the publishers. There's always pressure from the publishers."

My host was a writer famous for disdaining computers. The manuscript was in longhand and I was there, freshly educated and newly jobless, to type it up.

"I know your tutor well,' she continued. "Chris and I were at college together. Most of us scraped a degree, but he was always the academic. He recommended you as one of his best graduates. It's a great help, you being at a loose end. I only mentioned needing someone to Chris on the off chance."

"I'm glad of the opportunity."

After the meal, Kara showed me where everything was in the kitchen and gave me some housekeeping money. There was a small stock of cans in the cupboards and milk, butter, eggs, cheese and bacon in the fridge. There was also coffee, tea and a loaf of bread. Every expense had been spared with the coffee.

"I live in the grounds and I eat at home usually. You don't mind having to fend for yourself, do you? I'm afraid there's no TV, but there's one in the pub in the village. Mostly sport on, of course."

"No, I'll be fine."

~~~

I was drinking coffee and eating toast when Kara arrived to collect me in the morning. She was brisk, running at a different speed.

A makeshift office had been created for me in one of the unfurnished rooms above the garage. The floor was powdered with plaster dust and the smell of fresh paint was fumy and unpleasant. My desk was against the wall opposite the windows. The computer and printer were new. The cardboard boxes they had come in were stacked in a corner.

I had been delivered along with them, unpackaged, without a box. Cut and pasted in.

"Right," Kara said, waving for me to sit down and prepare to be instructed, "you'll find a photocopy of the manuscript in the drawer down there. Greg's handwriting isn't too bad, but it might take a little getting used to. Context should clear up most of the confusions. If it's not important take a guess. Anything major you'll have to clear with me. It'll be fine to correct any minor errors and misspellings. Greg will edit a hard copy of your draft and I can then amend the disc."

She bent toward me and smiled. "That clear?"

"Yes. I think so. I'll do my best."

"Good. Anything else you need?"

"It's a little cold in here."

"It is, isn't it," she said, rubbing her upper arms absent-mindedly as if this had just occurred to her. "I'll get you an electric fire."

She stopped in the doorway. "Take lunch whenever you like. But don't disappear for hours because we need you to crack on with this. You haven't got a car, have you?" she added with a frown.

"No."

"It's quite a long walk into the village. There are several bicycles downstairs in the garage – I don't suppose anyone will mind if you borrow one of them."

The manuscript was in a large box. It was perplexing at first glance because there were many crossings out and annotations. At least its amateur appearance was reassuringly democratic. It took some time to type up the first few pages, but the handwriting became easier to understand with familiarity. The opening of the book was compelling and it read smoothly, like the ideas had come quickly, intuitively. There were a number of small mistakes. I corrected them.

~ ~ ~

The sun was out at lunchtime and the grounds had an optimistic sparkle. As I cycled up the drive, I passed the old lady who opened the door yesterday walking back toward the house. I said hello and she smiled and lifted a hand without looking directly at me.

The pub in the village was quiet, a young couple sat eating by the fire and two older men in working clothes slouched comfortably over their pints at the bar like they had been installed along with the fixtures and fittings. The landlady, a sturdy woman of forty or so with greying fair hair and no make-up, wore a well-washed sweatshirt with the name of the pub on it. She nodded in a welcoming manner and appraised me briefly before coming over to take my order. Apart from this, I was left to eat my sandwich and drink my beer in a not unfriendly silence. The two men grunted a response to my goodbye as I got up to go.

I cycled up and down the main street before returning to the house. There was a post office and small supermarket, a river with a single arched bridge. The church was large and old, while the vicarage was a Victorian affair with a turret. For the most part the other houses were new and characterless.

~~~

After three days I had my routine. A morning of typing, lunch at the pub, a slower and sleepier afternoon. Sometimes I took a break and walked up and down or looked out of the window. There were peacocks in the grounds; they strutted about self-consciously like second-rate actors. Kara came across to check how I was getting on around five. She could not surprise me. The ticking of her heels on the cobbled courtyard was audible long before she reached the staircase. I liked her and we got on well. I had a feeling her visits were an opportunity for her to relax. We chatted about generalities and she sometimes read a little of what I had done.

I enjoyed my work. My host had set up a vivid situation at the beginning of the book, one dramatising a choice between bravery (and maybe foolishness) and rationality in a moment of possible self-sacrifice, the reader drawn in, complicit in the decision and challenged as a consequence. I was excited by where he was taking us. It was a powerful theme for a novel, both serious and pivotal. I tightened up a few less than elegant phrases, constructions showing signs of haste in the writing, unimportant stuff. They could always be changed back in the final edit if they were intrusive or unsuitable. I didn't think they would even be noticed.

I now knew the elderly lady to be Babs. She was Greg's mother. We talked for a couple of minutes one lunchtime in the garden. I wasn't certain she was entirely clear who I was and why I was there. I tried to explain, but she didn't appear greatly interested.

"Gregory's father would never have believed all of this," she told me, waving a hand in the direction of the parkland running down from the house to the river. "I don't quite believe it myself. We never dreamt of anything like this, you know, because it didn't seem a possibility in our world. Now I've come to take it a little bit for granted."

I wanted to tell her the truth, confess that I had dreamt of a place like this all of my life, but it would not have made her perceptions any the less real or genuine.

"Gregory is a good lad," she added. "We knew he would turn out well, even if it was only working in a bank."

~~~

Yesterday the TV cameras were here. Greg was doing an arts show interview to promote the coming
autobiography. There was a whole different feel to
the house, like it had been woken up, given a shake.
The sleepy corridors with their heavy curtains and
slightly damp smell were buzzy and bright. Deep-
voiced men, vigorous with expertise, were in and out
of the hallway all morning, ferrying equipment into
the study from the trio of TV vehicles parked in the
drive. An attractive girl with a clip-board and watch
liaised with Kara, their two heads bent over a sheaf
of crucial text banded with yellow highlighter.

I had been told to "keep out of the way."

I was beginning to get worried about the book. After the promising opening, Greg appeared to be suffering a failure of nerve. I could feel him wanting to
shuffle the theme of the novel away from the serious, and perhaps not easily answered, questions
posed by the very dramatic and original early
scenes. The subsequent chapters had taken on a
simpler, almost thriller-like structure and a stealthy
implausibility had begun to infiltrate the actions
and characterisation of the protagonist. I tried to
correct as much of this as I could, but I didn't think
I could pull it back to where it had been. Greg was a
runner true to form. His last three novels had
started brilliantly and then gradually fallen away
into something far less interesting and, to my mind,
not especially good. He had settled on a kind of
awkward cleverness, obvious in its issues and
prejudices, but most of all middle-class and safe.
They were books that complimented the reader into
thinking they were engaging with big topics while
delivering nothing of significance. All three novels

had been hugely popular and they had all won literary prizes.

~~~

I was picked up in the pub this lunchtime. I had eaten and the meal had left me replete and dreamy and not at all thrilled about cycling back to the house. I glanced around as I finished my drink and yawned. The bar had got a little busier and I noticed there was a girl at the table in the corner opposite me. A good-looking girl, very glossy and, you have to say, way out of my league. She had a glass of red wine in one hand and she was sipping while scanning a magazine. I watched her with the luxurious pleasure of the lonely man until she stopped turning the pages suddenly and looked up. This happened so unexpectedly, I was caught staring somewhat dreamily in her direction. My confusion and embarrassment, already mortifying, grew worse when she smiled. All I could do was smile in answer and return to my pint, gulping it down and hoping to make a tactful and prompt exit.

"Do you want a lift?" The girl, who now stood in front of me blocking my escape, held up a set of car keys and jangled them. "A lift, home to the house. You can put your bike in the back."

The bicycle went into the rear of the big 4x4 with ease. A half a dozen others would have found room there. The big leather seats positioned us high over the road, elevated above the mundane. Hope kicked off her shoes to drive.

"Kara said she'd get dad to introduce us, but the TV people were such a pain it all got forgotten. I saw you talking to gran in the grounds the other day. I was spying unseen."

"I haven't even met your father yet."

"Haven't you? How strange."

"I think he's had a lot on his plate as you say."

"Yes," Hope said distractedly, brushing back her long, dark hair. "I was going to pop up and see you in your hidey hole later. What do you think about the new opus? Ker-ching or not ker-ching?"

"I'm sure it'll do very well. Don't they always?"

Hope brushed back her hair again, a nervous habit perhaps. "Look is it all right if I drop you at the end of the drive? I've just remembered something I've promised to do."

~ ~ ~

I didn't see Hope that day or the next. Kara visited me the following morning, however, and we talked a little about the novel. She had been reading the pages I had already typed up and printed out.

"I'm enjoying it very much," she said. "It's quite different in tone to Greg's last few books. More like his earlier work."

"Yes."

"Do you like it?"

"Would it matter if I didn't?"

She laughed. "Not in the slightest. You met Hope, I hear," she added.

"She gave me a lift from the pub."

"She's a beautiful girl. Very like her mother."

I had wondered about the mother's absence. I took the opportunity to ask about it. It turned out to be a mistake, one of those conversation ending questions. A slight hesitation signalled Kara's decision to be on her way.

"Oh Lucy never comes down here," she said. "She prefers the house in London. Look, I'll have to be off. Have you got everything you need?"

"Yes."

"Keep up the good work."

~~~

Greg's work fell into two, very separate phases. Over the last twenty years he had inherited, or awarded himself, the role of the Great British Man of Letters. The author photo on his book jackets changed accordingly. He was now shown sitting at a large Victorian desk, face turned to the camera, a fountain pen in his hand. A picture of Dickens hung on the wall behind him. This was not at all how he began. When he first started writing, he was lauded as young and dangerous by the literary world, the kind of cosy iconoclast loved in this country, daring but not too daring. Nevertheless, he was good. In his attempts to avoid the intellectual, the traps of meaning and the Great Statement, he evolved a style that embraced the weird, the aberrant and the unsayable. His characters just acted and reacted, often in inexplicable and perverse ways, their mystery compelling. They had very little inner life and they were not located in society in any specific manner. As a young man, Greg had nothing to say, yet he said nothing with style and truthfulness. Any other approach would be dishonest, his work implied. Many young people felt as he did and he became their spokesman, a writer of his time, for his time.

~~~

Hope arrived as I was about to finish for the day. She poked her head around the door and scanned the room warily, a spy or a thief on the run.

I beckoned her in. "I won't bite."

50

"You flatter yourself. As if I'd be frightened of you."

"No?"

She frowned. "Are you pretending to be stupid?"

"Thanks."

"You're welcome."

"So who are you scared of?"

"Didn't want to bump into Cruella. And don't mistake revulsion for fear. I'll take on anyone."

"Cruella?"

She sat down on the edge of my desk and brushed back her hair. "Kara."

"You don't get on?"

"Christ, no. I'd burn her at the stake if I had my way. She'd return the favour, I'm sure."

"She is very protective of your father."

"Protective? Never heard it called that before. They've been banging away for years." She held up her hand. "No, I know, horrifying thought. Try not to picture it. I do."

"I didn't realise."

"Such a cliché, isn't it."

"I suppose so," I said, surprised by the observation.

The finished pages of Greg's manuscript lay in a box next to the computer. I had yet to replace the lid and put it away in the drawer. She lifted some of them and let them fall back slowly through her fingers.

"Writers are only ever original in their books, I'm afraid."

A thought occurred to me; an explanation. "Is that why your mother never comes down here?"

Hope laughed. "As if that would worry her. You don't know my ma. She'd kick Kara's tired old arse all the way up the drive if she gave a damn. But she hates it here. She hates my father. And, for once, he's in agreement, feeling exactly the same about her."

"I see," I said, not able to think of anything else to say.

"Do you? I wish I did."

~ ~ ~

I was coming to the end of the book. My earlier alterations had forced further edits and rewriting on me. One whole, rather silly, sub-plot had disappeared. One of the characters had been given much more to do, strengthening the backbone of the novel, maintaining a continuity with the brilliant opening, all of which belonged to Greg. I enjoyed the work, absorbed by it in a way I had never known before. Nothing else mattered. My only choice now was to see it through and then return to my life. Go back to the believable. Walk out through the door with the old-fashioned bell-pull. Walk up the drive, past the ornamental urns, the lawns and the shrubs. Walk away from it all and disappear once more.

~ ~ ~

Hope and I became friends over the next few days. At least, I became her friend and she tolerated me because I was there and she had little else to do. She was at home in that big house. She didn't see it, but she was part of it, a person of many rooms and possessions, surprised by nothing, demanding of everything by right. Her confidence was joyous, without limits, anarchic. I was warmed by it one minute and left shivering the next. I wanted to sleep with her, of course. Not just out of desire – although

I had a disturbing amount of that – but out of a
sense of becoming more myself in some, no doubt
perverse, way. She took me out to a restaurant to
meet her friends. It was an expensive place and everyone acted expensively. The friends, two other couples with very loud voices, weren't interested in me
and I wasn't interested in them. Hope wasn't interested in them either, but they seemed to expect this
of her. It was part of her power and they obviously
admired power. She had their esteem. Affection was
beside the point, perhaps.

~~~

The afternoon I finished the book, Kara came over to
see me. She was friendly, but I could tell my leaving
would simply be another tick on one of her lists.
Another problem out of the way.

"You've done well," she said, giving me an awkward little hug.

"We're very pleased with how quickly you've got
on. Tomorrow I'll print out another copy for Greg
and we can get on with finishing the book and get it
off to the editor. I'll expect Greg will want to see you
once he's looked it over and thank you. I'll sort out
your cheque."

Hope came up that evening and asked if I would
like to see her father's study. Kara and he had gone
out for a meal and would not be back until late. After some disagreement, I eventually said yes, not
because I was particularly curious about the place
where Greg did his writing, but because I wanted to
see her there, out of context, the writer's daughter
and proud.

It was a large, square room with white-painted
walls and two sets of French windows leading to the

terrace and garden. As the study of a famous novelist, its practicality and lack of pretension surprised me. A well-used sofa and two easy chairs in utilitarian grey were arranged around the wood-burning stove in the open fireplace. The desk and three filing cabinets were modern and commonplace – office furniture straight out of a catalogue. A rather unsightly old table with a liberal assortment of spirits on it and some glasses occupied the space between the windows. I am not certain why, but I had imagined oak-panelling and button leather chairs, something closer to a gentleman's club in a TV costume drama.

Hope waited with folded arms, watching me as I walked around the room. "Not what you expected?" she said when I stopped and looked at her. It was obvious she was laughing at me again.

"Not quite."

"You're a romantic."

"And you're a smug bitch."

"Oh I'm more kinds of a bitch than that."

Two of the walls were lined with bookshelves. All the standard works of reference were there, a vintage Britannica, Oxford dictionaries, several world atlases etc. Also a choice selection of fiction. I recognised many of my own favourites amongst the titles. One large section was given over to copies of Greg's work in translation, the first sign of pride so far, his very own tower of Babel.

Hope came and stood behind me as I examined the Japanese text in one of the books. "It's a long way, isn't it?" she said, looking over my shoulder.

"From here to Japan?" I said, turning.

She shook her head. "From someone you know, to someone who's known."

"You mean your father – understanding his fame?"

"What my father does is of no consequence to me. To who I am."

I wanted more than this from her. "It paid for all you have. That's something. It's a matter of respect."

She smiled at me and tapped my cheek with her fingers. "Do you respect your father?"

"Of course I do."

"Do you respect what he does?"

"That's different. He works in a factory."

"So did my grandfather."

"And you respect him more because of that?"

She brushed back her hair and turned away. "Maybe. At least as much, anyway."

I followed her over to the desk. It was very untidy. There were scraps of paper with doodles and smudged notes on them and a litter of pens and pencils, both new and old. The blotter was ringed with tea and coffee stains. A silver-framed photo of Hope as a child stood half-covered by the clutter. There was a slight crack in the glass.

Hope sat down in the chair and swivelled around to look at me. "You want to be a writer, then?"

"I've never said that to you."

"Sometimes not saying something, says something."

I held up my hand. "Spare me all that. You know fuck all about me."

"If you say so."

"What' s wrong with being a writer for that matter. You've grown up with the idea such a thing is possible. Some of us haven't been that lucky."

"Poor you," Hope said with a pout. She swung around on the chair to face the desk. "Your predictability is beginning to irritate me."

This stung. Nevertheless, I was not surprised by her contempt. It gave me a strange self-satisfaction. "I think I'd better go."

She laughed, but the sound cracked in her throat. It was clear she was upset. "Go. My chore is over. I was asked to look after you and that's what I've done."

"You were asked?"

"You'd have rather sat up in your room on your own every evening?"

"I thought you liked me."

"You thought what you wanted to think."

"I can't see you doing anything you don't want to."

"Really? I'm the dutiful daughter, you know." She shook her head and brushed back her hair with an angry flick. "But you don't know, do you. You're locked up inside. You don't see, you watch. You watch and you judge. That's what being a writer means, doesn't it? Judging and refusing to be judged."

~~~

I packed up stuff in the early hours and went downstairs. It would not have been wise to be around when Greg read his manuscript. I had given up on the idea of being paid long ago. I had done my job.

It was quieter to go out through the kitchen, but the light was on. I put my bag down in the corridor and peeked in. Greg's mother was sitting at the kitchen table polishing some cutlery.

"Come along, dear, don't worry about me," she said before I could duck back out of sight. "Just doing my bit to help. I don't sleep so well these days."

I picked up my bag and stepped into the room.

"Are you off? It's very late. Would like me to make you a cup of tea before you go?"

~ ~ ~

I had only been back home a week when the package arrived. It had been readdressed from my old college

"Feels like a book," my mother said, handing it to me over the breakfast table.

I was eating late and too well. My father had already gone off to work. I was being spoilt to a ridiculous extent at home, an oppression of kindnesses that felt both touching and annoyingly unearned. I was guilty because of this and angry to be so. Rightly ashamed of my ill-temper, I was careful not to show it.

It was a book – not Greg's new novel but the previous one, the one from two years before. Inside the front cover was a cheque for the sum we had agreed when I took on the job and a hand-written note. In it Greg thanked me and added, "Due to your speed and diligence, a bonus would have been in order, but, given the circumstances, I trust you'll forgive me for not including one. I suspect you have already read this book. Read it again and perhaps wonder that I managed to write it without your help. My daughter sends her regards. She tells me she thinks you're a good man. Such praise from her is a prize beyond rubies and emeralds, believe me."

The book was signed and dedicated. Underneath the dedication Greg had written out a quote from St Augustine:

"He that is not jealous is not in love."

Material

Marietta Burton murdered her husband and then wrote a best-selling novel about it. As she had written any number of books before, all of them with murders, all of them with husbands, she assumed no-one would notice . . . and they didn't. Killing people was her business. It was what she did best.

Of course, she disguised the circumstances slightly – she hadn't pushed Bill off an Italian cliff, she'd pushed him down the stairs – but in every other detail she told the truth about the murder instead of lies. In both fiction and fact the husband sent tumbling backwards with a half-swallowed yelp of surprise was a drinker, a frequenter of racetracks and a seducer of other men's wives, daughters and girlfriends. In neither instance was the deadly deed premeditated; in neither instance was it sincerely mourned. Bill went off to a better place and left a better place behind him. In both writing and life some things were inevitable even if they were unexpected.

To be honest, Marietta was secretly rather proud that she, a writer of detective stories, should have committed the perfect murder, even if she hadn't quite meant to. It gave additional psychological depth to her work if nothing else. And she liked the idea of the author as culprit, it was so apt, so accurate in essence. The writerhaddunit. Unfortunately, there was no way she could permit her fictional counterpart the advantage of such a perspective, or so sunny an outcome. Limited by the code of crime fiction, the wife in the story had no choice but to see getting away with the original murder as a mandate to carry out half a dozen more, no choice but to persevere diligently with gun, knife, poison and, in the final killing, a bust of Shakespeare, until Marietta's very own sleuth, Dr Patrick Maxim, was able to unmask her at around 85,000 words and thus bring the plot to a satisfactory conclusion.

Maxim knew all the answers, no motive was too slender, no method too tortuous. The only thing he had never been able to deduce was how much he looked like Bill. Marietta decided this was because she had imagined the pair of them.

Pointedly and a mystery in itself, although the book sold extremely well it was one of her least successful – perhaps because it was too clear a reminder to the reading public of just how conscientiously a woman could bear a grudge. Possibly it made both husbands and wives nervous, but for very different reasons.

Nevertheless, it was the only occasion anything to do with Bill that made money.

Noblesse Oblige

Carcellon castle boasted a prodigious cast of ghosts, ghouls and apparitions, but until the confrontation with his dead father Lord Palminter had never been haunted by any of them. Not even by Gory Breda the fingerless cook, an uncouth and, given the superior range of spooks on offer, exasperatingly ubiquitous spirit. Of course, he had been scolded never to admit in public to this sad lack of contact with the netherworld, supernatural goings on were far too good for business. In addition to what Palminter liked to believe were the castle's worthier attractions, the family provided ghost tours, ghost banquets, ghost nights, ghost challenges ("Stay the night, survive a fright – full English breakfast included"), anything and everything, in essence, that would generate a healthy stream of pounds, dollars, euros or yen. For the enjoyment of the visitors, the tour guides had even created a modern day ghost, a sightseer of generic foolishness (nationality fine-tuned so as not to offend against any patriotic feeling within the party being escorted) who had starved to death in a failed attempt to find their way out of the maze.

The old Lord Palminter, now three years deceased, had not been a popular man. Strangers disliked him on first acquaintance, while his household staff and tenants hated him from long experience. His family, compelled to tolerate his bad-temper and tyrannical stubbornness on an intimate basis, imagined themselves kindly disposed toward him on the days they did not wish him dead. Having inherited his title as a schoolboy of no great aptitude, the old devil's character had not been improved by the consequent indulgence of his every caprice. Only a saint or a psychotic person could have found it in themselves to excuse him his sins for more than a second without, at the very least, the encouragement of a warm sunny day, a win on the horses and several bottles of fine wine.

The old man had not been improved by death. He, contrary as ever, refused to haunt in a decent fashion. No Hamlet-like patrolling of the battlements for him, no dark portentous figure, no booming voice from the grave, nothing so dignified.

Now their children had left home, the current Lord Parminter and his wife Jane lived out a daily impasse of reciprocal discontent. He found himself on the wrong side of a conclusion she had come to about him at some point in their marriage, a conclusion that had the fixity of an established fact and was therefore undeserving of further discussion. He wanted to implore her forgiveness, explain that his pattern of indecision was not, as she obviously thought, a defect in his personality but a definition of it. He wanted to say this and yet, naturally, being British, he could never quite find the right time. As a consequence, he had now become ironical to and distanced from the one person who until now had always been on his side. Rather than be angry at him she affected a twinkling amusement at both his triumphs and his disappointments, the former few, the latter many. He, in turn, left the running of the castle to his wife and absented himself from her company as much as possible, working in the grounds under the instruction of the head gardener during the day and spending his evenings in his study drinking malt whisky with parched dedication and investigating his family history on the Internet. It was on one such evening that his father elected to add the insult of his resurrection to the injury of his life.

As a night it started inauspiciously. After climbing to the top of the east tower and entering his study, Parminter found a brightly-wrapped parcel on his desk. There was a handwritten card tucked under the ribbon. It read: "Darling, if you spend any more time where you are you will be needing this, if not now then later. Love, Jane." He frowned and ripped open the paper, revealing an antique chamber pot. A transfer print of a severe 19th century dignitary looked up at him from the bottom of the bowl, a re-viled politician, Parminter supposed, Gladstone, he suspected.

He propped the chamber pot up on its side next to his computer screen and poured himself a very large drink. "We find ourselves, at least metaphorically, in a similar situation," he said, toasting the face in the chamber pot and emptying the glass in one long, thirsty gulp. Gladstone glared back at him without pity. Parminter resorted to the whisky bottle once more. "What gives you the right to look at me like that?" he said.

The more he drank the more the face in the chamber pot appeared to scrutinise him and find him inadequate. Was it just his imagination or had

the politician's lips begun to curl slightly in contempt? A familiar expression, a painful memory
from the past he wanted very much to forget but
never could.

As Parminter bent nearer to examine the image's
mouth more closely, it opened in a black O and a
voice said, "I knew from the time you were a baby
you would turn out to be a useless article. Always
crying for the tit and frightened of the dark."

Parminter jumped back in shock and his glass
went spinning in the air, an arc of whisky flashing
golden in the light and pattering against the books
in the bookcase.

"I trust that's not my best malt you're throwing
around," the voice added. "Dry as the fucking Kala-
hari where I am now, damn it. Damn me in other
words."

Parminter rubbed his ears.

"Yes, it's me. You're not hearing things. Cause for
celebration, eh, you young pup. I don't bloody
think."

"Father . . .?"

The image at the bottom of the chamber pot was
the face of Gladstone no more. Red of eye, purple of
nose and curly of eyebrow, the late and greatly un-
missed Lord now glared across the desk at his son.

"But how?" said Parminter, blinking and shaking
his head as though to clear it.

"Never mind how. You wouldn't understand if I
told you."

"You're not a ghost. I never see ghosts . . . I must
be making you up."

The old Lord's burst of laughter broke up into a
violent coughing fit which went on until there were
tears running down his cheeks, the moisture col-
lecting in the curve of the pot.

"Are you all right?" asked Parminter.

"Of course, I'm not all right. I'm bloody dead."

"So you are," said Partminter after examining the situation and coming rather too cheerfully to a conclusion. "No need to worry, then."

The old Lord scowled. "Don't get insolent with me, laddie. You might still have something approximate to a life, but somehow you've managed to make a god-awful fuck-up of it."

"And you're the expert on well-led lives, are you?"

"Well, your mother didn't have me gelded and stabled, I can say that at least."

"And often did," said Parminter, getting down on his knees to look for his glass. His laughter was muffled as he reached in between the desk and bookcase to retrieve it. "There were plenty who'd gladly have offered to hold you down, if she'd just said the word."

The old Lord snorted. "There wasn't a soul amongst you who had the guts."

"Or the wish to soil their hands. I never understood how you could carry on behaving so revoltingly day after day knowing how much everybody despised you."

"Everybody? Who gives a bald bugger about everybody? Everybody can go hang. The only thing I ever cared a fig about was this house and preserving the family history. You've come from greatness, lad, and don't you forget it."

Parminter refilled his glass and took a sip. "Yes, I've been looking into the deeds of our illustrious family. Much to be proud of, it's true, but what about the rest? What about the generations of wasters and gamblers and womanisers?"

"Drunkards, too," said the old Lord, "don't leave them out. Don't get picky and flatter yourself."

Parminter snatched up the chamber pot and made for the window.

"Break the pot you'll never be rid of me," the old Lord warned with a bark of surprise as he was whisked away from the desk, his voice echoing around the porcelain. "I'll be part of this place forever. A ghost you bloody-well will be able to hear and see and that's a promise."

The chamber pot returned to its place beside the computer screen, Parminter refreshed himself with a mouthful of whisky and said with a sigh of irritation, "Okay, so what do you want?"

"That's more like it. We can do business now."

"I doubt that. But say what you have to say."

"I want my last wish."

"Contracts with the devil are that generous now, are they?" said Parminter with mordant satisfaction. "You get the luxury of last wishes in your sizzling new abode? Doesn't appear likely. Especially in your case."

"Everybody gets to have a last wish. Mine is a little different, however. It's been quite complicated to organise."

"So what do you want from us? I don't imagine your last wish expresses any sort of sentimental attachment to your family."

"Certainly not," said the old Lord with a grunt. "What a notion. The whole worthless bunch of you were nothing but an encumbrance weighing me down. You in particular. You have proved a disgrace to your name, a weakling and a democrat and a dishonour to the noble title bestowed on you by blood."

Parminter laughed. "Now you're the one resorting to flattery. Thank you, anyway."

"I'm glad you think it's so damn funny. If you

don't assist me I'm going to enjoy sticking around here and making the rest of your life one long penance."

"Now that I do believe. So what's the wish?"

"I want to drive the D-Type one more time."

The D-Type Jaguar was one of a collection of performance cars the old Lord had raced in his younger days. They were now displayed in a small museum in the old stable block. The old Lord was forced to give up his career as a racing driver when his competition licence was revoked for deliberately running another driver off the track in a manoeuvre that threatened to be fatal. Fortunately, the challenger survived with a few broken limbs and a story for his old age.

"I see," said Parminter after a pause. "You've surprised me. Sit in your old Jag." He sipped his drink and then shrugged. "Fine by me. Sentiment of a sort. I'm almost willing to say I might have misjudged you."

"Sentiment? I knew you wouldn't understand," said the old Lord with a sigh of exasperation.

"Hmm, yes, you're right, perhaps it's better that way."

"You're as clueless as ever, but as long as you agree to help I don't give a hoot."

"Why not? Happy to get off so easily. Shall I put you on the driver's seat?"

"I can't drive a car from the bottom of a potty, you idiot."

Parminter laughed. "Well this is all nonsense, isn't it. You can't drive a car from anywhere these days. Anyway, the Jag isn't roadworthy and the petrol tank is empty."

"You don't say? What a pity. Better just give up, then, I suppose?" The old Lord shook his head in disgust. "I might have known you'd try that one. Well, you're a liar as well as a fool. I happen to know that you rented it out to a film company last week and it's fuelled up and in perfect working order."

Parminter was nonplussed. "How did you find that out?"

"I know everything you know."

"You can't."

"But I do."

"How? How can you possibly know that?"

"I'll let you figure that out. It won't be too difficult. So is it a yes? I need you to say yes. Just the one word."

"One word?"

"Yes."

"Yes? What good will that . . ."

The old Lord smiled in triumph and his face began to blur in the bottom of the chamber pot.

Parminter opened his mouth to speak, but got no further, a great elbowing inrush of energy knocking the wind right out of his lungs. As he gasped for breath, a blossoming nimbus of light expanded to fill the space around him, the paintings on the walls glowing brighter, the desk and the computer screen, the titles on the spines of the books on the shelves and the detail on the furniture snapping into a new and emphatic sharpness. He had known this room since he was a child, it was completely familiar to him, but now, in an instant, he knew what it was to own every part of it, to own everything beyond it, every ancient and precious gift that had been passed down to him. For the first time in his life he was cleansed of doubt. The castle was his. It belonged to him and no-one else.

Without wanting to he found himself searching for the spare keys to the motor museum and the Jag in his desk. Once he had them he got up and hurried downstairs, an unwilling passenger on his own legs. He did not wish to go, but here he was going.

Jane alerted by his quick footsteps coming down the stairs and, curious about the novelty of him stirring from his study in the evening, intercepted him in the hallway.

"You're not going out?" she said.

"I most certainly am," Parminter heard himself say in a peevish tone that was familiar but certainly not his own.

"Not driving in your condition, I hope."

"My condition? What on earth do you mean woman?"

"You're drunk. Very drunk if your mood is anything to go by."

"Don't be impertinent. And get out of my way."

The expression of dismay and disbelief on Jane's face was a vision so sweet it begged to be recalled and played back at a later date. Stunned and open-mouthed, she stood aside.

His legs then carried him to the castle's great door, where his hands worked the great lock and his feet swept him off into the dark night air. As he was taken across the courtyard toward the gatehouse, he could sense Jane watching him as she stood on the castle steps in the light from the hallway.

At the motor museum, Parminter looked on as he rolled back the tall sliding doors. Inside, he was propelled summarily into the open cockpit of the Jag, fitting into it as if it had been made for him. He continued to watch as the key found the ignition. How could this be happening? He had never even sat in the car before, never driven anything faster than his old Land Rover Defender or Jane's Volvo estate.

The big engine cleared its throat, coughed, back-fired and then ripped into deafening life. Before Parminter could resist himself he had slammed the Jag into gear and sent it out through the doors with a squealing of rubber. The power of the car's acceleration kicked him back in his seat. He tried to move his foot to brake at the turn on to the castle's long drive, but it stayed hard on the gas. The bend flung him from side to side in his seat and the rear of the car wagged hideously, straightening just in time to make the corner.

The Jag touched 90 miles an hour as it approached the lodge and the main gates. Fortunately, the ticket office for the castle was in the car-park and the gates remained open until the autumn when the house closed to visitors. The car shot through the ornamented stone pillars and up to the T-junction, slithering to a halt with a shriek of tyres. After the merest blink of a glance back and forth at the empty road beyond, it was foot down and off again in the direction of the village.

The speedometer needle flickered around the 120 mark as the Jag reached the glow of the streetlights on the outskirts of Carcellon village. Despite his fear and desperation, Parminter had to admire the skilfulness of his braking and gear-changing as they screamed down the narrow streets lined with old stone and half-timbered houses, the monstrous snarl of the big cat's engine echoing off the walls. The Jag slowed to a sedate 60 miles an hour as they came to the one-way system. Roker, one of the shopkeepers who supplied the castle restaurant, was walking up Market Street. He rocked on his heels as the car hurtled past him, seeing a wide-eyed Lord of the manor at the wheel. Parminter wanted to make some sort of sign, wave a hand or shout something to the man to absolve himself of blame, but when he lifted his hand it flashed two fingers in a vee and when he opened his mouth all that came out was a roar of coarse laughter not his own.

The Jag did two circuits of the Market Square, burning rubber on the tight turn around the old Corn Exchange. Parminter recognised two members of the Parish Council sitting outside the wine bar at the far end of the square. One of the teachers from the local school turned to see what was going on as he was about to go into the Thai restaurant with his wife. On the way out of the village, the Jag grazed the old corduroy of Sam the poacher's trousers as he wobbled home from the pub on his bicycle. Parminter looked in the car's wing mirror and witnessed Sam unseated in a spectacular windmilling of arms and legs, but he could do nothing.

At some point later, Parminter came to and realised he and the Jag had returned to the castle motor museum. The engine was off and, apart from a faint residue of exhilaration, he felt safe. A protracted sigh that did not belong to him escaped from his lips and his hands, no longer strangers to him, began to shake.

Thankfully, Jane had gone to bed when Parminter crept back into the castle on trembling legs. The place felt old and dark and distanced from him once more. His lack of belief in castles and ancient rights and noble blood comforted him as he ascended the great staircase. Back to the gardens tomorrow, he said to himself. Back to the gardens to hide and hope for the best. Maybe he had imagined the entire episode?

The old house was quiet, any ghost present encouragingly unseen. When he reached his study he poured himself a large scotch. It wasn't until it was almost finished that he had the nerve to look into the chamber pot. Gladstone had returned. Relief washed down through the young Lord Parminter's bones. He put the pot on his chair and, staring at the distinguished prime-minister's stern features, felt an abrupt, and humbly human, urge to pee.

Above the splashing of urine as it swirled satisfyingly against the porcelain, Parminter heard a loud cough. Glancing over his shoulder, he saw Jane waiting by the door. She was in her nightdress and dressing-gown and her eyebrows were raised. She shook her head in pity.

"The police are here to see you," she said with all the smugness of someone who has won an argument not just for a day but forever.

Not Funny

Comedian Dave Daniels stopped being funny at 9.30pm on Tuesday the 4th of August 2005. Live on the night at the Bradley Theatre, he died on his arse. Toothache or a tax demand would have cheered the audience more than he did. Every one of his punch-lines missed, striking nothing but empty air. He felt picked on by the spotlight, lit up in his distress, jealous of those in the darkness beyond for the first time in his life. The microphone grew slippery as a fish in his hand. His tongue tasted of sand.

At the end of the gig, the boos and catcalls chased him out through the stage door and across the carpark. When he gained the silence of his car they got in beside him. Take us home, they said.

His third marriage failed later that week. He packed up and walked out when his wife, Zanda, said, "Let's face it, DD, there are more important things in this world than making other people laugh."

Stripped of his time on stage his life lacked punctuation, rhythm, culmination, appreciation. Days dawned without zest, lingered sombrely and ineffectually, then faded away into darkness. Funny things didn't happen to him on the way to anywhere. The only person who walked into a bar was him. The solitary thing he could time with any certainty was his breakfast egg.

He sought professional help, paid out serious money. He told the psychiatrist of his anger and resentment at the joy he saw other comics giving to an audience. "A-*penis* envy," diagnosed the doctor with a smile.

Even his therapist was wittier than he was.

He had money. He didn't need a job. None of his three wives were after him for their keep and his investments over the years had been lucky or perhaps even wise. To fill the hours, he volunteered for an unpaid position as a porter at the hospital near his new home. The hard work and suffering calmed him. He was appropriate. Days on the wards were too real for the traffic rushing by on streets outside, too absolute for show-biz, for stand-up and bright lights. It was a world in parentheses. Nothing was expected, everything was hoped for.

After a while he began to forget who he had once been. What he once was and had lost. He became useful again, a role choosing him. His bad jokes, filling the long silences with words, were received by patients and their families with gratitude and inattention. No-one expected him to be funny. Funny had no place in this world.

Kindness had come late to him.

Life sometimes went on.

Picking

We marched by a Belgian girl picking cherries on our way back to the Front. She was caught in a bar of sunlight beneath the branches, the glow around her setting her apart amongst the shadows like a moment remembered. A little piece of the past that patch of light seemed to me at the time, her white apron and bonnet still bright as we left her behind, the straps of out rifles cutting into our shoulders as our boots slipped on the rutted road.

My father is the gardener at the manor house in our village. I used to help him pick the cherries when I was a little boy. Help was how he described it, but mostly I just helped myself to the crop. I love cherries more than any other fruit to this day.

There's no way to deny it, my dad is sometimes an angry man. He seeks perfection in everything he does and he expects the same from the lads that work for him and his family. He doesn't bestow a happy expression on the world easily. I have things to do, is what's written on his features when he's about his business, and you should have the same. I do not think this is always what's in his heart. Often when I used to speak with innocence or without thinking as a child, he would laugh and a tender look would momentarily soften his face before becoming a frown, the feeling in him so fiercely resisted it was almost like he was in pain.

Not even the high-born and mighty are spared my father's anger. On one occasion – a memory that is more than precious to me now – I was witness to him losing his temper with the master. The two of us were picking cherries when the master's dogs, Dicken and Dan, arrived at a gallop. I was pleased to see them as they were my good friends and, as always, they greeted me as if I'd been mislaid and then found and needed to be loved all over with leaps and licks. The master came striding along in their wake, spruce in his tweeds and swinging his stick as if he were fit to take on an army or two.

"How goes it, Sam?" he says. "Good year, I'd say."

"Not bad, sir," says my father. "You'll not go wanting, that's for sure."

"Got your little chip with you, I see."

"Aye, he's keeping an eye on the proceedings."

"How are you young man?' the master says to me. "Are you going to grow up strong and join your father in his noble trade?"

"He's right enough," says my father, seeing I was too scared to open my mouth and find what might come out."

"The scamp seems to be eating more than he's harvesting. Damn me, I'll have no cherries left if he has his way," says the master, not unkindly and smiling all the while.

My father froze in his picking and frowned. He descended the ladder in a slow and deliberate manner. Putting down his basket, he turned to the master with his hands on his hips.

"I'll gladly pay you for anything the boy eats, sir," he says, his chin high and his eyes staring with pride and without deference into the master's. "You may deduct the sum from my wages."

"Now, now, Sam," says the master. "I meant no harm. I was just ragging the boy. He can eat his fill."

My father nodded, his anger given up grudgingly. "That's as maybe. And thank you, sir. But mark my words, I'll have no-one taking this time from the lad. He'll be breaking his back for kindness and his keep soon enough. There won't be anyone to give him anything. He'll have to do what he's told and go where he's sent. Right now, he has the certainty of my two capable arms and his mother's care. Later, it might not be so."

My mother and my two sisters came to the station to see me off after I had joined up and received my orders. Dad would have none of it. "I'll not raise a farewell hand at your going away," he told me. "Time enough for sentiment when you come home safe and fit to work. I'm a gardener, a nurturer of plants and trees, what do I want to know of wars and soldiering?"

But as the train pulled out from the platform and I looked away from my mother and Joan and Sarah crying and waving their handkerchiefs, I caught a glimpse of a familiar figure in a worn cap and Norfolk jacket standing at the stile on the hill below the big house. He was still standing there as the carriages rounded the bend and all I had ever known until that day began to disappear from sight.

Place de l'Europe

Photographer Henri Cartier-Bresson stole the moment, clicked the shutter on the scene: the posters on the wall, the silhouette of the spectator, the train-track of the makeshift ladder partially bridging the water, the hurrying man in the trilby hat, legs scissored, suspended in air, a blur caught in the speculum of the puddle.

~ ~ ~

Fernand felt the chicken shift beneath his arm as he splashed down a whole metre short of dry land. He cursed yet ran on. Sabine the hen, buttoned-up inside his jacket, clucked in commiseration. His poor old shoe had a hole in it and his sock was wet through – but he deserved nothing better.

He reached his destination ten minutes later, out of breath and, he was sure, quite likely out of luck. But no, he halted with a squelch on the pavement under Aimée's window. The afternoon was overcast and there was a light on. It warmed his imagination as he entered the building. The hallway was dark and smelt of old vegetable soup and cats. As he went up the stairs complained beneath his feet like a worn-out bed on Saturday night.

It took several determined knocks on Aimée's dirty blue door before there were sounds of movement inside. A further hearty thump resulted in the door opening an inch, one hard yet beautiful brown eye peering out at Fernand.

Aimée was not at all pleased to see him. "Not you again," she said. "Go away. The Comte will be here soon. Come back tomorrow."

The Comte was Aimée's gentleman friend. People called him the Comte because of his expensive black suit and the carnation he always wore in his buttonhole, but he was only a society tailor's third assistant. It was costing him most of his salary to keep Aimée in clothes and out of them.

"I have something for you," Fernand said.

Aimée's grip on the door relaxed a little. "A gift?"

"Yes. Can I come in?"

"Where is it? I can't see anything."

"It's inside my coat."

"Show me."

"Not in the hallway."

"I hope you're not being disgusting."

Fernand was aggrieved. "Have I ever given you cause to think I'm that kind of man?"

Aimée hesitated then stood back and let him in. The small shabby room was brightened somewhat with dusty-looking Arab rugs and silk hangings. The bed was wide, barely leaving space for a dressing table and stool and two frayed easy chairs. There was a strong, slightly sour smell of face powder and perfume. Fernand took a deep breath and his head spun with familiarity and contentment. How he loved it here. His eyes turned to the bed. In the lamplight, the yellow coverlet glowed a welcome. His legs felt unsteady as he held his jacket tightly closed.

"Well?" Aimée said, folding her arms and looking Fernand up and down. She was wearing Turkish slippers and a thin red robe in the Chinese style. Two large embroidered peacocks faced each other across her breasts, their feathers iridescent blue and gold.

Fernand opened his jacket and released a sleepy Sabine on to the back of one of the chairs. She clucked sceptically and looked around the room. A blink of her polished amber eye took in Aimée's hand as it came toward her and she jumped down on to the floor with a loud squawk just in time to avoid it.

"Get that filthy thing off my furniture," said Aimée, squawking in harmony. "What the devil do you think you're doing? Bringing a chicken here. Whatever next? A pig? A cow?"

"It's a very rare and special chicken," said Fernand, picking Sabine up and stroking her feathers.

"Who cares. What do you imagine I am, some kitchen maid?"

"You could buy a brand new automobile with the money she cost."

Aimée narrowed her eyes and looked at Fernand doubtfully. When he refused to be stared into submission she leant forward, head to one side, and inspected a nervous Sabine with reluctant curiosity. "Looks like a plain old farmyard hen. And no better than a boiler, if you ask me."

Fernand clasped the hen tighter and drew it away as though to save it from further insults. "She's a white Cathay. A bird bred to perfection for thousands of years by the greatest and most powerful emperors of China."

Aimée shrugged. "A chicken's a chicken. Why would anyone want to do that?"

"You don't think she's beautiful?"

"No, I do not. She looks tatty and her feathers are all muddy."

"That only proves that you know nothing about chickens," said Fernand with a sad shake of his head.

"Indeed it does. And what's more I don't want to. Which leads me to wonder why you brought the horrible thing here? What did you expect me to do with it?"

Fernand held up his hand. "Now don't get angry."

"I will if I want to."

"Of course. But . . ."

"But what?"

"Well," Fernand took off his hat, "I thought that you and I might possibly . . . you know."

"You know what?" said Aimée, tightening the belt on her robe impatiently.

Fernand nodded toward the yellow glow of the bed

and pressed his hat against his chest in reverence. Sabine clucked in sympathy under his arm. "Er . . . Come to some sort of accommodation?"

Aimée's eyes widened alarmingly and she let out a shriek. "You expect me to sleep with you for a chicken! A chicken! You think that's all I'm worth? Are you mad? Why do you insult me in this way?"

"She's a very expensive chicken. You can sell her for a large sum," said Fernand speaking quietly and reasonably and making a calming gesture with his hat.

"Then why don't you sell her and come back with the money?"

"Unfortunately I cannot. It's a question of time ..."

Aimée laughed despite her anger. "Your need is that great. There are plenty of women on the street who'd relieve you for a few francs. Go to one of them."

"But they are not you, Aimée. It is you I must have."

"Me?" said Aimée, softening a little. "You must have me?"

"I must. I've risked everything for you. This chicken is my wife's favourite chicken."

"I'm not surprised if it's worth what you say it is. You should both sell it and become rich."

Fernand nodded, his expression sad. "I want to, but the bird was given to my wife by her father and she will not be parted from it."

"And yet you want to give it to me," said Aimée, laughing. "Your story does not make sense. You must think me very stupid."

"But if the chicken disappears and I am none the richer, my wife will not suspect me of any wrongdoing."

"Why not hide the money? Spend it over time."

Fernand shook his head. "You are a woman. If you were a married man you would know better than to suggest such a plan. A wife will know from your very walk, your very smile, that you have funds you have kept to yourself."

"And sleeping with me won't make you happy? Right now I think you should be paying me compliments."

"Sleeping with you will make me ecstatic," said Fernand, raising his voice and stroking Sabine with more passion. "Haven't I proved to you that I'm willing risk everything?"

Aimée narrowed her eyes. "I'm not so sure of that. What will happen to you if your wife finds out what you've done?"

"Do not," said Fernand, his face white as Sabine's feathers, "make me even think such a thing. My life is miserable, but happily so. If my wife finds out what has happened to her favourite chicken, I might as well be dead."

"Dead?" said Aimée, beginning to look alarmed.

"Dead," said Fernand with priestly solemnity.

Aimée said nothing for a moment and then appeared to make up her mind. "Just this once, then," she said, untying her robe, "but if you ever come here again with such crazy story I'll have the Comte beat you to a pulp."

Fernand thrust Sabine in Aimée's direction. "Thank you, thank you," he said. "May you be blessed for taking pity on a poor man."

Aimée yelped and drew back. "And you can take that filthy thing away with you." Dropping the robe, she walked to the bed. "Come on, be quick, I haven't got all day."

"Certainly, Aimée," said Fernand, placing Sabine on the chair, "I will take care of the task in hand with as much speed as possible."

~ ~ ~

Bernice, Fernand's wife, was in the kitchen when he returned home. She was putting a pot on the stove. Her sleeves were rolled up and her face was flushed with the heat. She was a good-looking woman with dark hair and a strong body. Bernice's father had once told Fernand that his daughter had wrestled a pig to the ground for a bet.

Fernand kissed her on the cheek. "Hello, my sweet."

"You're a little late."

"I am, my dear. Sorry. I had a rush job to do."

"They should pay you more. You let them take advantage of your good nature."

Fernand shrugged and took off his hat and coat.

"Have you seen Sabine?" said Bernice. "I can't find her anywhere. She's getting old now and the eggs are getting scare. Time for her to go in the pot."

"Really? I just passed her in the yard. She must have been under the shed. You know she likes it under there."

"Well I looked, but it was too dark to see anything." Bernice moved to the door. "I'll go and see to her, then."

"Yes," said Fernand, a little distracted. "No wait. You don't think we could have fish tonight, do you? Sabine seemed so happy scratching in the dust. It isn't much to ask of a life, after all."

"No, I suppose not."

"I hate to say it, but I appear to have grown quite attached to her."

The Dainsford Lofty Column

Greetings postulants to the church of discernment! Welcome to my book-lined study and my book-lined mind. Breathe in the odours of old leather and foxed vellum. Forgive the undertones of musty corduroy and wet Labrador. I trust that you, like me, have a balloon of the finest five star Napoleon close at hand and that your buttocks still smart, if only metaphorically, from the lash of nanny's slipper. There are logs on the fire and the servants, wretched in their ignorance, are safely below stairs in front of the television.

My subject for today is originality. Oh, how sorely we have suffered of late from the mediocre and the hackneyed. As Will Shakespeare should have said: "Let not history blunt thy bodkin and custom cloud thine orbs." Where is the sear of the new, the gut-rip of the innovatory, the brutal uppercut of the bold and the uncompromising? A book might ensnare the emotions, give wise council, evoke feelings of common humanity, use irony and humour to comment wittily and perceptively on contemporary mores, but where, I ask you, is the Art in that? Philistines crowd in on all sides and the true artist is left gasping for the air of public acknowledgement. My admirable friend Dicken Slump's new work, The Scab of Passion, an elliptical tale of a depressive microbiologist's love for the bacterium that bears his name told without capital letters and employing random vowel substitutions, cannot find a publisher. How can this be? The man is a prose stylist of incomparable incomprehensibility. His principles are not to be doubted: on being told by a reader that his work was "rather enjoyable" he shed tears for a week and then attempted suicide (a period in his life he is, at this very moment, transmuting into fiction).

Alas, the time has come for me to extinguish my cigar and cap my fountain pen. I have a rubber suit and dog-leash to slip into before the magnificent Madame Badger, my therapist, arrives; already, dear friends, I tremble in anticipation of her spike heels click-clicking along the draughty marble corridors of my psyche. Afterwards, I have several dozen volumes of literature to absorb before supper-time. Three in Latin, one in Greek, two in a particularly piquant Eastonian patois, the rest in conversational (ah, the lure of light reading) French and German. I wish you, my loyal fellow scribes, a much worse time in the future and I trust your muse will permit you to pass on just a little of your misery to the rest of us in your writing.

Sky Child

Ida Croft, Sky Child, felt for remembered hand-holds with the tips of her fingers and swung herself across from Crooked Ledge to Broken Tooth in one confident movement. Crooked Ledge to Broken Tooth was the hardest and almost the highest part of the climb. Far beneath her feet, the cliff fell away to sharp rocks and sand.

It was a warm day and the sun burnt her shoulders, her shirt wet against her skin. She wiped her forehead and clenched her fist in accomplishment as she stepped into the shade of the gully. Without pausing, she picked her way up it to the top. A new section of the overhang had crumbled since her last ascent, eight years and a World War ago.

The grass was cool and green in the shelter of the monastery wall. Ida lay down in it and closed her eyes. It was good to be back. Good to hear the sea and the gulls and the beating of her own heart. She felt safe in a way she hadn't for a long time, a true part of this familiar, resonant world. A dog barked on the beach below and a man's voice called after it, "Fetch Shadow, fetch it, boy."

~~~

Her cousin Sigmund let her in. The great oak doors groaned a welcome, weary on their hinges. A powdering of dust fell from the stone arch above like frost from a wind-blown branch and both Sigmund and Ida coughed. The monastery represented the largest part of the patrimony of the Oldacres, Ida's mother's family, a home to the eldest son since Henry VIII levelled the chapel and part of the cloister in 1538, cruelly dispossessing the holy brothers with an armoured toe.

Ida's uncle Marius and his son and daughter, Sigmund and Octavia, were the current trustees of the ancient key.

Ida had driven up with her mama in their old Ford two days before. Mama was off to a wedding up in Scotland. "Why don't you change your mind and come with me? You'll enjoy it," Ida's mama had said, stopping the car outside the monastery.

"Why would I?" Ida replied.

"You'll be married yourself one day."

"How do you know that?"

"Every girl wants to get married, darling."

"I'm not every girl."

So Ida had been left to relive her holidays at the monastery as a young girl. It was a month past her seventeenth birthday, June 1947.

"Father is 48 not out in the refectory," said Sigmund. He had been a rather nice-looking boy of nineteen before the war. A ground shift of grief and lost innocence had seemingly undermined one side of his face during military service, the slippage dragging down his left eye and twisting his prominent nose out of symmetry.

Sigmund loped ahead down the long stone corridor. It was as though he didn't want to be seen with Ida. She was forced to speak to the back of his neck.

"Octavia should try a leg-break. Her bowling's far too easy to read."

Her cousin didn't answer. It wasn't until they reached the refectory that he turned a drooping eye over his shoulder. "Why are you dressed like a boy?" he said.

"I'm not. I'm wearing trousers. Women do these days."

"What's wrong with a skirt?"

"I've been climbing the cliff. Do you remember how you taught me the way up? Showed me The Chimney, Crooked Ledge and Broken tooth."

"No."

Uncle Marius held up a hand in greeting and quickly returned to patting his bat against the stone flags of the refectory floor, eyes alert and intent. Octavia huffed on the ball and polished it with her handkerchief. A look of theatrical aggression distorted her beautiful face as she trotted toward her father and brought her arm up over her head. The energy of her delivery loosened a tendril of her intricately-sculpted hair. Fast but too straight, the ball bounced just where Marius was expecting it to and he stepped up to the wicket and slogged it high into the air.

Ida dodged around Sigmund without taking her eyes off the ball and ran to the far end of the refectory, where she turned, cupped her hands and took the catch with ease. It was difficult not to smile in triumph as she walked back up the long room, but such displays were bad-mannered. Octavia had gone to her father's side. Sigmund stayed by the door, where he stood winding his watch and whistling silently.

"Well held, sir," said uncle Marius, unable to look Ida in the eye, his show of good sportsmanship tempered with a black scowl. When Octavia tried to console him, he threw down his bat and kicked it across the floor. "Damn it all, bloody fool, never could resist a sitter."

~ ~ ~

They all went to the beach that afternoon, descending the steep stones steps in procession. Ida carried a hamper made up by cook, Sigmund carried his father's cane chair and Octavia carried a large red, white and blue parasol. Uncle Marius insisted on taking the lead, awkward on his absurdly long legs and obstructively tentative in picking his way to the bottom. One of Octavia's wide-brimmed sun hats sat on the very top of his huge head. The monastery rats had apparently eaten his straw boater.

Marius sat in his cane chair under the parasol with a dusty bottle of stout from a remote corner of the monastery cellar and a tobacco-less pipe. Ida and her cousins walked out to the sea's edge. Octavia was contentedly over-dressed in her tailored-suit and full make-up. Sigmund had on one of his father's cricket jumpers and a pair of voluminous army shorts. His feet were bare and white and completely without hair. They made Ida think of the pale creatures fished up from the dark of the deepest oceans.

"We're flat broke and father won't do a thing about it," Sigmund said.

Octavia was impatient with this. "Don't listen to him, Ida. Father does his best. He was on the phone to his stock-broker just the other day."

"Everyone's feeling the pinch," Ida said, turning her face up to the sun.

"The war has bankrupted the country and us,"

said Sigmund. "But I have some ideas and father won't listen to me."

At lunchtime, Ida, Octavia and Sigmund put down towels and sat on the sand around Marius's chair. The hamper open for business, they all toiled away at thick Spam sandwiches cut from crusty bread and drank strong dark tea.

"Got a job lot of this stuff from the Yank commander over at the airfield," said Marius, munching immensely with his long jaw. "Did a swap with him for one of those ghastly brown paintings on the wall of the chapter-house. A minor work by some Venetian artisan or other."

Octavia swallowed with difficulty. "It doesn't taste too bad when you get used to it."

"It's perfectly edible," said Ida. "I've eaten much worse. The bread is fresh at least."

Sigmund had already finished eating. He brushed the crumbs from his lap and lay back with his hands behind his head. "Cook bakes every day when we have the flour."

Marius took a long draining gulp of tea and wiped his moustache on his sleeve. He turned to Ida. "So how have you and your mother been, Sky Child . . . does my sister still call you Sky Child?"

"No." This was not quite true, but Ida would have preferred it to be.

Marius sighed. "We were on this very beach all those years ago. Do you remember?"

"Not really."

"You and Sigmund came back from climbing on the rocks and your mother asked you what made you want to get to the top so badly."

"I was very young," said Ida. "When you're young you say things."

"And you said, 'To go all the way up to the sky.'"

~ ~ ~

Octavia's bedroom was next door to Ida's. Her cousin stood at an ironing-board in a pink negligee, pressing her underwear. She worked swiftly and neatly, a trance-like expression on her face.

"I've just come in to say goodnight," said Ida.

Octavia looked up in surprise. "Oh Ida, yes, sorry." She shook her head as if to clear it. "I was in a dream."

"I get like that when I'm climbing."

"You do? Isn't that dangerous?"

"Do you burn yourself when you're ironing?"

"No, of course not." She thought for a moment and then nodded. "Ah, right, I see what you mean."

Ida picked up one of silky frilled items in the basket on the bed. It was cold and slippery and she let it fall back through her fingers. "Do you always iron your underwear?" she asked.

Octavia had taken off her make-up and her face shone soft and young in the lamplight. Her eyes widened. "Don't you?"

"No, I've never thought of doing it."

"You haven't?"

"No. Of course, I don't have anything nearly so fine."

This seemed to please Octavia. She ironed on with renewed energy. "What if your horse rolls on you?"

"I'm sorry?" said Ida, blinking in puzzlement.

"What if your horse rolls on you and they have to take you off to hospital and the doctors, you know . . ." She made a vague gesture with her free hand in the region of her more intimate areas.

"See your wrinkled smalls?"

"Yes."

"That would worry you?"

"Very much. Wouldn't it you?"

"Not at all. Anyway, I haven't got a horse."

Octavia rested the iron. "Nor have I," she said with a wistful glance at the window and dark night beyond. "We can't afford the upkeep. I do have a motorcycle, though. I take father on the back when he wants to go to the races."

Ida frowned. "Uncle Marius can't afford to go to the races, surely?"

"Oh he doesn't bet. He says he likes the noise and the colour and the smell."

"And you?"

"Me? God no. I hate the smell."

"Not that. What do you like? You're always so well turned out, Octavia."

"It would be nice to have a place in London. Nice, to be able to go out at night to the theatre or a restaurant or a dance."

"Yes. Strange, I can do things like that at any time, but I never do."

"Not ever."

Ida felt guilty. "Afraid not," she said, avoiding the pain in her cousin's eyes. "Don't you have a boyfriend or anything?"

"No, not any more. There was Vivian. He was in the Household Cavalry. We were going to elope together and live in sin. But then he was killed in the war."

Ida put her hand on her cousin's arm. "I'm so sorry. I'm certain he was very brave."

"He was," said Octavia, a gem of a teardrop sparkling on her cheek. "That is he would have been. Unfortunately, he was run over in the blackout on his way back from a Knightsbridge brothel."

~~~

There was toast and homemade jam for breakfast. They sat on benches at one end of the long table near the south wall of the refectory. The big doors to the outside were wide to the sun. Octavia and Sigmund deferred to their father when serving themselves and Ida followed their lead. Marius placed the poignant wedge of toenail-coloured cheddar cheese close to his elbow and scoffed it all with a majestic lack of remorse. His bald head had a polished sheen and his two remaining tufts of grey hair stuck out from behind his ears. Ida, Octavia and Sigmund were dressed, but he was still wearing turquoise silk pyjamas under his too-small plaid dressing gown, the sleeves at half-mast.

The mood at the table was subdued. Ida had come down to breakfast a little after the others. When she arrived Marius and Sigmund were arguing over Sigmund's proposal that Marius should go to his bank manager and ask for a loan to pay for the necessary structural repairs to the monastery and for replanting the gardens. All of this in preparation for opening the house and grounds to the public.

Marius was unimpressed. "This is my home not a bloody museum."

"It's what we need to do to survive," said Sigmund, spooning jam from the jam-pot on to the side of his plate with a little too much vigour. "We've no money and no other way of getting any."

"I have my stocks and shares."

"And how much do they bring in? And on top of that I need something to do and Octavia shouldn't be wasting her time here. She needs a place in London."

"No, I don't," said Octavia, her voice rising in protest. "I want to stay here and look after father."

"Liar," said Sigmund, staring aggressively at his

toast and then biting into it noisily.

"I'm not."

"Of course you are. Look at you. You're all dolled up like a Hollywood siren and the only chaps who get to see you are father and I. Bloody waste if you ask me."

"Places in London don't come cheap," said Marius with a pugnacious thrust of his chin.

"Exactly," said Sigmund.

Not a word was exchanged for several long minutes after this, the mood at the table stormy.

As a non-combatant, Ida felt duty bound to change the subject. "I want to climb Oldacre's Mace," she said. Oldacre's Mace was a tall rock stack rising out of the sea a few miles down the coast.

"Why on earth would you want to do that?" said her Uncle Marius.

"Do I need a reason?" said Ida with a shrug.

"I rather think you do, young lady."

"There's the treasure," said Sigmund.

Ida sat forward. "Treasure?"

"Eldrick Oldacre supposedly secreted the family gold and jewels on top of the Mace during the Civil War. Seems he was frightened of ending up on the wrong side and losing everything."

"Will that do?" said Ida, turning to her uncle.

"The whole idea is absurd," said Marius. "Much too dangerous. And you're a . . ." He gestured at the front of her shirt with his spoon, "well, you know . . ."

Ida looked down and then up with a scowl. "Not a man?"

"Why shouldn't she do it?" said Sigmund, a little too quickly, the ill will obvious in his voice. Ida knew his motives were suspect, but she was glad of his help all the same.

"Yes, why shouldn't I?" she said. "Sigmund can come with me."

Marius laughed. "Sigmund takes after me. No head for heights at all."

"Rubbish," said Sigmund. "Heights don't bother me in the slightest."

"There's no shame in it," said Marius in an appeasing tone. "Your uncle, Ida's father – God rest his soul – was an adventurer, dead at thirty-five in a fast car."

"Daddy! Please," said Octavia, sitting back in shock. "Think of poor Ida's feelings."

Ida turned and squeezed her cousin's hand. "That's all right, Octavia. I was just a baby when he was killed. Never really knew the man."

"True, true," said Marius. "Reckless lot the Crofts. Everyone knows that."

"You're not keeping your tactlessness much of a secret either, father," said Sigmund.

Marius wasn't listening. He shook his head. "You're my son, Sigmund. An Oldacre. You take after me. Love cricket and having your feet firmly on the ground. Quite right, too."

"I loathe cricket," said Sigmund, getting up from the table.

"No you don't," said his father clapping his hands rubbing his palms together as though this was an end to it, "you love it."

~~~

Ida was lying on the cloister lawn reading when Sigmund found her. She hadn't seen him since the argument that morning. He seemed more animated than usual.

"Good book?" he said, sitting down beside her on

the grass.

"Bit of a bore, actually," said Ida.

The sad half of Sigmund's face seemed to expect something of the sort. A trace of a smile flickered elsewhere. "Did you mean what you said about wanting to climb Oldacre's Mace.

"I always mean what I say."

Sigmund nodded. "Right. Yes. Totally. Are you game to do it tomorrow? Weather permitting, of course."

~~~

Oldacre's Mace was six or seven miles along the coast from the monastery. Ida followed their plan and breakfasted early the next morning and waited for Sigmund in the village. When he came careering dangerously around the corner on Octavia's ancient motorbike, she jumped on to the pillion with a yell and they zigzagged off up the road.

Ida waited while Sigmund hid the motorbike in the gorse on the cliff above the Mace. As he bent to cover the machine, the intense yellow of the flowers briefly warmed the sad grey of his skin. Task accomplished, he motioned for Ida to follow and set off at a vigorous pace. So vigorous, she had to run to catch up with him. He lingered at the top of the steep downward path. It was low tide and the saw-like promontory linking the beach with the Mace was exposed. The column was lit by a soft, misty sun, golden in the light and a deep blue in the shadows. Ida had reduced the elevation of the stack in her imagination. The hundred feet she remembered was over a hundred and fifty in reality.

"It's a different shape," she said.

Sigmund nodded. "A section of the summit broke off."

"It looks more like a seated man wearing a bowler hat than a mace."

"Such is history," said Sigmund with something that might almost have been a laugh. He turned and started the descent.

The sea ka-boomed against the rocks, a boiling of foam and jade green. It took time and all of Ida's patience to reach the stack, the crossing broken and slippery, bright with deep pools. At the base they halted and looked up. Ida was a little frightened by what she saw, by the dark shape excluding the sky, too big to even notice her, but fear made her angry and anger made her stubborn. She imagined the light on her face when they reached the top, the elation at having defeated the world and herself.

She turned and looked at her cousin. "Doesn't seem all that bad," she said, her throat dry. She coughed to clear it.

"It isn't when you know the way up," said Sigmund, his sad eye watching for her reaction.

Ida was suitably puzzled. "You've spoken to someone?"

"No, I don't need to. I've climbed the Mace many times."

"I don't understand," said Ida, shaking her head. "Why didn't you say?"

"You didn't ask."

"I thought you'd lost interest in climbing."

"I have. The last time I was here was before the war."

Ida followed Sigmund around to the seaward side of the stack. He pointed out the route. "I tried to get to the top several times before I got it right."

"But you didn't find the treasure?"

"There is no treasure."

"If there isn't," said Ida folding her arms and looking hard at her cousin, "why would people say there is?"

"It's a story, Ida. Just a story. With treasure or without treasure, which version would you prefer to hear?"

Ida thought for a moment and then laughed. "With."

The climb went well until Ida reached a ledge six or seven feet beneath the summit of the Mace. She held on tightly, the sea-breeze bringing tears to her eyes, and risked a look down at the water exploding into spray on the rocks more than a hundred and forty feet below, daring the view to make her giddy. The way had been comparatively easy thus far, the route one of solid hand and footholds even if it did appear tortuously indirect at first glance. Without Sigmund's lead Ida would never have found the way. He reached the top and appeared over the edge when she called out to him, the pull of gravity causing his drooping face to droop further still.

"What's the matter?" he said.

"I can't stretch up the last bit. I'm too short."

Sigmund seemed numb. "Oh. Right. Damn. Didn't think of that."

"You'll have to help me."

"Help you?" Sigmund's reply was almost a squeak.

"Yes. Reach down and give me your hand."

"I can't," Sigmund protested, shaking his head.

Ida didn't want to fail right at the last. "Of course you can," she said, anger in her voice.

"What if I'm not strong enough? What if you fall?"

"I trust you."

"You do?"

"Of course."

Sigmund said nothing for several seconds and then, with a painful sigh, he reached down and gave

Ida his hand. She grasped it firmly and offered up a prayer to her father. The footing was uncertain, but after searching around with her toe and swinging out momentarily over the sheer drop she eventually found some purchase. As she scrambled inelegantly up the slippery rock and over the lip, she saw her cousin's face relax, his one sad eye shining brighter than she had ever seen before.

The top of the stack was a thick, flat slab almost square in outline. It was much bigger than Ida had anticipated, its contours and fissures smoothed off by wind and rain. She smiled in conquest and ran her fingertips over the rock and then, crawling away from the edge, lay back exhausted with her arms and legs spread wide. With a grunt of agreement, Sigmund did the same and stretched out at her hip. They both looked up at the cloudless blue sky, at the seagulls diving and weaving.

"You're very brave," Sigmund said.

His voice sounded disembodied, the words tugged at by the wind. Only the birds are above us, thought Ida. We might as well be flying. We have risen up so far from what is real. Left it behind. This is our freedom. "It's what I want to be," she said.

Sigmund was silent for a moment. Finally, he said, "Yes, I see. I think I understand."

"You got through the war. That's true bravery. I was scared by the bombs."

Sigmund laughed, his body shaking with the sudden violent rush of it. Ida, taken by surprise, wondered if he would ever stop. "Oh dear," he said, eventually getting his breath back.

"Are you all right?" asked Ida.

"Yes. Sorry. I know what you're saying. The bombs scared the stuffing out of us, too. Along with the bullets, the shells, the landmines, the tanks, the planes and every now and then even each other."

Ida didn't like being made to feel young. "I didn't mean it like that."

"No, I know," said Sigmund, his voice kind.

"Still the war must seem a million miles away on a day like today."

Sigmund grunted and shifted uncomfortably. It was as if his bones were hurting him. "You would imagine so, wouldn't you. But in Italy we had so many fine days, the sky blue, the sun hot, birds singing, the countryside beautiful. The craziness of it all was harder to bear on days like that. At least it was for me. It was easier when the weather seemed in tune with the war, dark, cold, wet and hostile. Fine days tricked you, made you imagine a time when the fighting and killing would be over. Losing someone you've lived with for months on end, risked your life with, who's become a friend in such a setting isn't just tragic it's an insult."

"Yes," said Ida in a whisper.

"We were billeted in a derelict villa on the coast at one time. There was a terrace overlooking the sea. Must have been a lovely place before the shells hit. My sergeant had found a couple of bottles of wine and we were sitting outside in the sun having a drink when a German Stuka came up over the headland and strafed us. Larner, a good friend of mine, was right next to me and he took a bullet in the head. Killed him outright. He was still smiling at a joke someone had told."

Ida shook her head. "That's terrible."

"I was his commanding officer. My responsibility was to take care of my men, yet the first thing I felt was a thrill of joy. I was so glad it hadn't been me."

"To feel that on top of everything else," she said, reading his expression.

"You understand?"

"Yes."

"It wasn't about the loss of someone in my unit, of a friend. That came later."

"Who have you told about this?"

"Just you."

"Not Marius?"

"No."

"Octavia?"

"No-one."

"They've never asked you about the war?"

"They've asked, but I've never told them. It doesn't seem to fit here."

"No, I suppose not. But you do."

"Oh yes. I do."

They both fell silent. The wind had grown stronger and it now sang in the crevices and crannies of the Mace. A herring gull flew low over them, the updraft ruffling its wing feathers. Its yellow eye and the dab of red on its beak were plainly visible.

Sigmund sat up and looked at his watch. "Time we were leaving."

"Right," said Ida with a yawn.

"I'll need to give you a hand down."

"You will."

"I won't drop you."

"I know."

"You can trust me."

"I can and I will."

"Thank you," said Sigmund, his sad eye glinting as he smiled.

"I'll remember this day."

"So will I."

"We looked down on everything."

Sigmund sighed. "I'm going to have to sort out father and the future of the Monastery once and for all."

"You are."

~ ~ ~

Sigmund was adding something to his list of things
to do when Ida came back to the refectory after
speaking to her mama on the phone.

"All fixed?" he asked.

"Yes. She'll be here on Friday, old Ford permitting." Ida sat down and poured herself some more
coffee. She nodded at the list. "You're going to be
busy with all that lot."

"At least with the bank loan agreed and papa and
Octavia out of the picture I can get underway."

Uncle Marius and Octavia had left earlier that
morning. Bill Bennett from the village took them to
the station in his van. Octavia's luggage only just
fitted into the back. Uncle Marius, dressed in his
blazer and flannels, made do with a single soft can-
vas bag, his favourite cricket bat slotted between the
handles. He was going to stay at his London club
while they carried out the work on the monastery
and gardens. Octavia had a rent-free room in a flat
in Park Lane owned by an old school friend. She
hoped to study acting and go to dances.

Octavia wept and kissed Sigmund and Ida fra-
grantly as Bill got into the van and started the engine. But there was a smile on her mouth as she
took her seat and began to retouch her lipstick. Uncle Marius shook hands with them rather grudgingly.

"If this turns into a bloody disaster, I'll hit your
bollocks right over long on," he told his son. "It's
against my better judgement, you know. All sorts of
riff-raff traipsing around the place."

The monastery was quieter than ever now they had gone. As quiet, indeed, as a monastery should be. There was no sound of high-heels tapping along the cloister or dance music playing loudly late into the night. No sound of leather on willow echoing down the celebrated corridors. No sound of Uncle Marius bellowing for cook to get a damn move on or farting loudly in the stairwell and then laughing.

Sigmund added one last item to his list and put away his pen. His sad eye shone in the sunlight from the open door and his skin was no longer pale.

"I believe you'll make a really excellent job of this place," Ida said to him.

He smiled. "I'm glad to hear that."

Ida stretched and got up. "Time for one last look," she said.

~~~

It was another clear blue morning. Ida stood on the cliff-top and drew in a deep, sweet breath. Up above, a bright red aeroplane grew larger and larger, its engine buzzing. As it dropped down to roar low over Ida's head, it waggled its wings. She loved the noise and speed of it and, closing her eyes, she could see what the pilot could see, a girl alone, head thrown back, hair blown by the wind.

Somewhere Else

Liam walked down the hill from the rented cottage and along by the churchyard wall. He felt a pinprick bite on his ear and looked up. A column of gnats hung over him in the evening air like an unclear thought.

Opposite the village green, several youngsters were skateboarding down the sloping concrete apron in front of the pub, aiming themselves at one another and only changing course at the very last moment. The lone girl taking part dipped and swerved with particular grace, redistributing her weight with fluid movements of her arms, hips and feet, her pony-tailed ringlets flying. She reminded Liam of a girl surfer he and Justine had watched in Cornwall the September before. How envious he had been of the way the girl laughed to herself as she splashed out of the ocean and walked back up the beach, her eyebrows and lips white with sea-salt. After dropping her board on the sand, she shook her arms and legs in a shivering dance, shouting out that the water was "Tit-freezing cold." It hadn't been easy to look away from the elastic curves of her wet suit, the long zip an invitation – drawing it down like peeling a fruit.

"So all the tales about men in middle-age are true," Justine teased him later, having followed his eyes. "I want to make it absolutely clear that I won't wear rubber for you no matter how nicely you ask."

The village telephone-box was of the old-fashioned sort, the exterior pitted and scabbed with layer upon layer of red paint. Its battered appearance and survival into another time seemed almost stubborn. Perhaps there was a kind of liberty in being overlooked, in being allowed your own history, your own lost world? Opening the door, he remembered the Japanese soldier who, when rescued from a lonely Pacific island twenty years after VJ-Day, refused to believe that the war was over and his country had been defeated.

Even on a summer evening the box's interior was redolent of urine and wet wool, of shelter on dark, rainy days. There was a dead matchstick, a *Kit-Kat* wrapper and a wizened brown apple-core on the shelf beside the receiver. On the floor there was a sooty mark where somebody (the parish pyromaniac?) had unaccountably tried to build a fire.

"Oh it's you," Justine answered. The disdain in her voice sounded vengeful, a weapon readied in advance.

"Don't get too enthusiastic, now," he said.

"I won't."

"Expecting a more attractive offer, is that it?"

"And you'd care, I suppose."

Liam stepped back into the life he used to live. He asked how her preparation for the new teaching term was progressing; if there had been a call or letter from Davy; how she was coping with the bills; if the garden was getting overrun; whether her car was going okay. As he spoke, he listened to what he was saying as a stranger might listen. It was eerie, the feeling of being on the outside, at a distance, eerier yet to discover he was able to talk across that distance. Here was here and there was there.

Justine's replies were listless, resentful. "Feel easier now, do you?" she said when his questions began to falter. "Feel everything at home is all right so you can go on exactly as you are, go on treating me the way you're treating me? I don't have to stand for this, you know. I might be a fool for you, but I'm not a fool. If you think I don't have what it takes to carry on on my own then you're wrong. If I have to manage I will, so don't kid yourself on that score. You never know, keep on as you are and you could well find there's nothing for you to come back to."

Liam allowed her to run on, to get it all out. "None of what's gone on has been about you," he said when she had finished. "You know that."

"Thanks a lot."

"Don't pretend to misunderstand. I feel bad enough as it is."

"Do you?"

"You've been very patient."

Her laughter was bitter. "What choice have I had."

"I'm sorry."

"Are you?"

"How can you ask that?"

His certainty seemed to take her by surprise. There was a pause.

"What's wrong?" he asked.

"You sound different," she said.

"Do I?"

"Yes. More in control."

It was Liam's turn to laugh now.

"Does that mean you're not?" she said.

"Perhaps."

Justine sighed to herself. "You haven't got three wishes. You're who you are now. Nothing stays the same. You'll have to come to terms with it eventually," she said.

"I know."

"You agree?"

"Of course I do. I'm not stupid."

There was another pause.

"Are you still there?" Liam asked.

"Yes."

"You've gone very quiet."

The Bracelet

Lester bought Paulette a silver and turquoise bracelet on their final holiday together, a trip to the States. "Created by Native American craftsmen," it said on the back.

While driving across New Mexico they had pulled off at a store with a tepee and campfire outside. Picturing the scene, he could still taste the burnt earth sucked into the air-conditioned Chrysler when he opened his door to the sun. The interior of the store was ice-box cool. On a sound system a country boy was singing: "*You left your panties in my pick-up and your heel-print on my heart.*" The air was pungent with pine and tanned leather, the stock overflowing into the aisles and under the feet. Behind the ranks of cowboy boots, saddles and Stetsons, the jewellery hung on knuckled tree boughs, the stones like big blue insects, the chains like bright Spanish moss. On learning they were from the UK, the bald man at the cash register – the topographical undulations of his hairless scalp given a varnished gleam by a baby spotlight above the counter – began to reminisce about being based at Mildenhall with the USAF.

"Mostly it was okay," he said. "Sure, things sometimes got a little out of control. You British people don't always make it clear what's expected. If a guy don't know that, he can stir up all kinds of trouble for himself without exactly meaning to." He unsnapped the sleeve of his fancy western shirt to reveal the knife wound he had sustained in a late-night fight in Ipswich city centre. The scar ran up in a long sweeping arc on the inside of his forearm, white against his dark skin like a seam of quartz. "When folks here find out I got cut in England they think I'm putting them on," he protested. "Now if old Robin Hood had shot me with an arrow it'd be different."

Paulette had laughed when they were back in the car, her new bracelet jingling as she grasped the key to start the engine. She said the scar was probably the result of some sort of agricultural accident. Lester listened from the passenger seat, the abrupt changes in temperature having converted his tiredness into a headache. Paulette gave the windscreen a wash and wipe as they accelerated from the car-park. Dust exploded into dark rivulets on the smoked glass, the sky beyond clean and polished, pure as a beginning. The grille of the Jeep Cherokee on a dais at the front of the adjacent car-lot flashed in the sun. A yellow VW Beetle with two pairs of skis tied to its roof-rack passed them going in the opposite direction. There were what looked like bullet holes in the sign at the edge of town; beyond it the road was deserted once again.

On The Corner of Moon Street

Jimmer is my brother in truth rather than blood. Blood dries into dust and can be blown away. The truth of a life lived in trust is like stone. It was good to hear his voice again. Back when we were living and working on the corner of Moon Street, it was my anchor against the tide, a certainty to hold on to, to know and keep close. To introduce him to Rosette, my bride and companion, and have the two of them in the same room together, all of us with full stomachs and close by a warm fire, has long been my desire and earnest ambition. He was much taken with my wife, as I knew he would be, and I could tell she approved of my old friend Jim Costerman in return by the teasing nature of her replies.

Jimmer and me met on the streets of East London when we were lost lads. I was singing for a piecrust outside the pub called the Hoop and Stick, a bad pitch he was desperate enough to think of as his own. A fact he informed me of loudly with a shove for good luck. But his voice softened when he realised I could not get myself right side up from where I had fallen without reaching for the wall. Because I was born into the dark and remain so until this day. A blind beggar boy, they Christened me when they turned away or chased me off – just in case I should forget who I was. Not that I cared, it was all I knew and I could draw no margin between who I was and what I was called.

"How do you stop sharp boys around here from a-stealing the money in your cap?" he asked after lending me a hand up and brushing me down.

"I takes me foot off when I feels a shift in air from the toss of the coin and stamps it back down arter I hears the ching," I told him.

Jimmer plays the violin real sweet and sometimes he dances. We liked each other's skills and dispositions so well we made a partnership of it after that first day. I would sing as nice as any choirboy and Jim would bow his fiddle and turn a figure or two. Save for in their need and their hunger, no-one cast out on to the streets is entirely whole. Jimmer has a wooden leg and a boldness that wins over or humbles any who would laugh at him. The applause and the coppers in our hat were proof enough he was as nimble as the best despite his misfortune. He lost his limb to a man-trap laid by some fine gentleman's gamekeeper. He and his poor father were poaching for the table at the time. What happened to his dad after they were caught, Jimmer never did find out. Put on a ship to the colonies and said farewell to appears most likely.

We inherited our spot on the corner of Moon Street after our friend the puppet man passed on. A place we defended against our foes like a fortress. At night we would wrap ourselves around each other in the blanket I wore across my shoulders during the day without shame or false pride. The butcher's doorway was our home and alley cats and rats were our companions. All of us feral and doing the best that we could. Jimmer and me became well-known in the neighbourhood and sometimes gathered a crowd. Most paid up readily and some did not. The did nots had their own consciences to trouble them. What was worse were those that blubbed into their nose-rags at our travail and kept their hands tight in their pockets. For you cannot drink another's tears or spread sympathy on a loaf.

One day a tough old lady smelling of soap and sanctity took hold of me by the hand and would not let go. She and her strong boys saw off Jim and dragged me away to blind school, where I was done good to and made respectable. Taught to grow up and play and tune pianos, I was, and very grateful for it in the end. Met my Rosette there, the two of us sharing the darkness yet finding the light of each other. Sharing the words and emotions for these things, that is.

Jimmer went on to become a second-biller on the Music Hall stage. His violin playing famous for its accuracy and pathos. I was told about his act when he was booked into the Pavilion Theatre here in our seaside town and I recognised Jim from his name and his attributes. I think there was much feeling on both sides when we met again in his dressing room. But we stayed manly and shook hands, despite my Rosette's weeping.

Jimmer stayed with us that night and left early the next morning to get back to London. I still had not slept when Rosette came down.

"Did you play all night?" she asked.

"We did," I told her.

"And did you recall old times."

"We did."

"You must be tired."

"I've never felt less sleepy in my life, my dear."

What I wanted to explain to her, yet could not, was that, when it comes to what I once was and what I once knew, there is no escape from memory nor any sincere wish on my behalf to do so. For some reason I was both cast down by fate and honoured by it and there is no way to unravel the two contingences.

Jimmer and me lived day by day and minute by minute back then. We had no future and dreamt of none. We worked and slept on the corner of Moon Street and in some hidden fibre of us we always will. Always.

"We were saved," I said to him as we refreshed ourselves with a glass of beer between tunes, each one a reminiscence and a celebration.

"Like sinners on a Sunday," he replied.

"No, not sinners. Like mariners shipwrecked by storms not of our making."

He laughed and sawed a few notes of a sailor's hornpipe on his fiddle. "And hearty enough we are tonight with our ale and good company. Me with me peg-leg. You with eyes that will see no ships."

The Egg

Sophie turns the Fabergé egg in the glow of the lamp on the bedside table whenever she is sad. Its beauty and absurdity cupped in the nest of her hands, jewel points of light reflecting in her eyes.

The egg has to be a fake, reality doesn't allow – my reality doesn't allow – such grandeur to exist in any world shared by Sophie and I. Because she would not keep a treasure of this kind in a drawer where even the stupidest burglar might easily come across it, now would she? When I asked her why it wasn't in a bank vault where it belonged, she said there could be no value, no joy in appreciation, without risk. To truthfully own something priceless, she said, you have to live with the possibility it might be taken from you at any moment. Put a diamond away in a locked room and all you possess is a key.

Over sixty eggs were made in Peter Carl Fabergé's workshops in St Petersburg, the majority of them for the Russian royal family. Sophie's egg is mauve enamel, the kind with a surface shimmer to it, and there are cross bands of gold set with diamonds and rubies. It opens to reveal three miniature portraits, two ladies in evening dress and a man in uniform with a beard. Romanovs, I imagine. With a nod of approval and pride, Sophie says all three appear dignified yet humble. I see nothing but their lack of doubt.

Sophie's family have large houses and little money. She inherited the egg from her great uncle Leo. The lawyer handed it over in a chamois leather bag with a scarlet drawstring. No mention was made of the contents of the bag in the will. This much Sophie has told me. But Sophie lies all the time. She often declares herself bored by the truth. She wants to have fun and she feels the truth is something she should not have to put up with or acknowledge. Sophie lies to me because she knows untruth makes me anxious. She taunts me like someone who is not afraid of heights might taunt someone who is. She stands on the edge of all I believe in and thrusts an arm and a leg out into space, pretends she is about to tumble headlong. I fear for our safety and she laughs at the drop.

Sophie's sadness is no lie. It comes upon her in the early hours, just before dawn brings light to the sky. She will not share it with me. It is hers alone. I can only watch and wait for her to return.

In nature, a hen's egg is a simple wonder, elegant in proportion and symmetry, clean of line and forgoing any craftsman's adornment. It is merely what it is. It is precious in conception and execution without being in any way unique or valuable. It is a welcome gift for a hungry man yet almost nothing for a king . . . or perhaps a queen, a sad queen. It might be as real as the hand that holds it, but for all its truth and honesty it sparks no light.

The Fire

As a boy, Patrick watched a house burn to the ground. A beautiful old house – Georgian it must have been. Until a few months before the fire, he delivered newspapers there (*The Times* and *The Daily Telegraph*, the one house on his round that took them), wondering as he wheeled his bike up the path what it must be like to live in so large a place, to not have to share a bedroom, to never have to worry about making too much noise and upsetting the neighbours. He would recall the early morning smell of the garden, lavender, mock-orange, tea roses, herbs, a lawn wet with dew. The sign on the gate said Manor Farm, but the farm had gone years before, the land sold off to build the council estate that Patrick and all his friends lived on.

Following the death of the farmer, the house and out-buildings were scheduled to be demolished and new homes for senior citizens put up in their place. But the local kids, Patrick amongst them, pre-empted this by breaking in and taking the place apart, smashing the windows, digging away at the damp, sandy plaster and pulling down the banisters and doors and setting light to them in the trampled remains of the garden.

The older boys returned one night to frighten themselves, exploring the rubble-filled rooms on the ground floor, hot candle wax dripping on their fingers, long-limbed silhouettes dancing on the walls. At the foot of the ruined staircase they pushed and collided with one another, whispering dares until one of them was brave enough to lead the way. Above, they had already imagined a ghost haunting the attic – a witchy hag in a mouldering white dress, her beckoning finger long and bony. Up they went, so scared to see things that they saw things. On the top landing, one of them pointed into the shadows and shouted a warning and they all clattered back down, falling over each other in a breathless tumble.

The rest of the house had been ripped open and stripped of the past, but the attic kept something to itself. Even in daylight, going up there made Patrick uneasy. The door leading to it was closet-sized and disguised as a panel. You had to insert yourself through it, ducking down and straddling a high threshold. The steps were narrow, enclosed, your shoes booming on the bare boards. They came up in the middle of the room, the attic revealed at floor-level, surrounding you with shadowy corners, three more than you could take in at a glance.

The atmosphere was suffocating under the eaves. Patrick remembered the taste of dust in his mouth, the itch of it in his eyes and nose. The warmer it grew, the more it stank of bats and mice and bird-shit. There was a dead baby bird at the top of the stairs, a monstrous thing with a bulging head and transparent grey flesh.

The only light came from four round dormers set north, south, east, west in the roof. At certain times

of the day the sun would shine in through the win-
dowpanes and create a golden-moted cross in the
air above the stairwell. That was what the other kids
insisted, anyway, their heathen eyes widening as
they passed the image around. A cross, just hanging
there. Like a sign. Like Dracula.

A few days before the blaze, someone laid a large
elegant turd at the top of the stairs, the curl of it
serpentine, tapering, flies a buzz of shimmering blue
as you approached.

Patrick and his friends never found out who
started the fire. No-one would confess. No-one
would laugh guiltily when questioned. Somebody
said they had seen some older lads in a car earlier
that evening. It was too easy an explanation and not
much believed.

By the time night fell, the house was alight from
front-door to chimney-pot. The whole estate congre-
gated to watch, a ring of mums and dads, small
children in dressing-gowns, old people with their
teeth out, teenagers smoking surreptitiously, hands
cupped behind their backs. The heat when the roof
gave way buffeted the crowd like a breaker on a
beach, sparks exploding heavenward in the dark,
the in-rush of air transmuting what was left of the
building into a roaring skull.

Three weeks later, they bull-dozed the ruins into a
pyramid of scorched brick and charcoaled timbers.
A year later, there were fifteen bungalows and a
block of single-bedroom flats on the spot. Twenty
years later, the block of flats (constructed from
bolted-together concrete slabs, the building suffered
with leaks and condensation the council could never
cure) was pulled down and replaced with a toddlers'
playground.

The Flower and the Bee

I lived with the great Mercal Mercali for many years. Sometimes she would take me to her bed, the wondrous actuality of her body as nothing when compared with the limitless cornucopia of her acting talent.

"Think of yourself as the flower," she whispered in my ear on one occasion. We were lying in the moth-eaten squalor of her four-poster, its canopy supported on a quartet of cankerous fairground horses. "I'll be the bee," she added.

"Shouldn't it be the other way around?" I replied.

"You flatter yourself," she said.

"If I don't, no-one else will."

She smiled. "Yet more self-abuse, Paul. Time to give up on the truth, it will always find you out."

Mercal and I met as students at the Central School of Drama. We were friends then lovers, then lovers who were friends, then – our careers having taken separate paths – voices on the phone. A decade later, when Mercal was internationally famous and I was not, she accepted the role of ministering angel after the failure of my first marriage and the fading of her third and offered me sanctuary and a large room in the attic of her Hampstead house. Somehow over the years I forgot to leave.

In the short interludes when Mercal was not working and I was taking a rest from the soap opera ('drama serial,' the TV company called it) that had become my bread if not my butter, we sometimes spent time together. Stardom, with its assumptions of excessive individuality, continually demanded from her new and more flamboyant displays of eccentricity. The gurus and the religious questing, the mad, often dangerous, health regimes, the dungaree and shaven-headed old feminism giving way to the fairy flounces and tumbling curls of the new. All this made her interesting to herself and, I admit, to me. She liked to pretend she was at the mercy of her own surprises, unexpected in both her tastes and her beliefs, but there was something cold-blooded about the way she persisted with her adventures and experiments. She would not be boring or bored and there was an end to it. What other people did or put up with were not part of her reality. Boring and bored might be out there, but they were not possible or even feasible in the universe she inhabited. It was her duty to deny them, a duty that came with the job.

Mercal did surprise me on one occasion, however. We were sitting drinking a suitably disgusting vitamin supplement next to the rock pool in her newest addition to the house, a large Victorian-style conservatory glazed with green glass and landscaped with jungle foliage. I was not able to catch what she was saying at first because of the splashing of the waterfall.

"What?" I said, pushing away my almost full glass with a finality I hoped would be noticed and not questioned.

"My son," she had raised her voice, but only a little, "will be coming to stay with us for a while tomorrow."

I sat forward in my chair. "Your who?"

"My son. I don't think you've met."

"Wouldn't I have to know of his existence for that to happen?"

She thought about this. "True," she said with a nod before returning to her drink.

"How old is this son?"

"Eighteen."

"And the father?"

"Benoit."

"The film director?"

"What can I say. It was hot, the film was not good, we were stuck out in a remote village in Africa with bugger all to do in the evening. I was young. Human sexuality abhors a vacuum. Benoit had a mind as well as a body. Much less work in the afterglow. I'm sure we both seemed attractive at the time."

"And where has the boy been for the last eighteen years?"

"With his father's family in northern France and then at a Public School in Wiltshire. He comes into the city sometimes and we meet up at the Ivy for lunch."

"But he's never been here?"

"To the house? No. He's never expressed any interest until now."

"It's difficult to imagine you as a mother."

She sighed. "Yes, I'm tragically un-maternal."

"Are you looking forward to seeing him?"

"Good god, no. I never look forward to seeing anyone."

"You're such a democrat. So what are we going to do today?"

Mercal frowned meditatively and stirred the murky liquid in her glass with her finger, which she then licked. "Let's go to the coast and eat fish and chips and paddle in the sea."

"Your car or mine?"

"My car's faster."

"Mine's less ostentatious."

"Definitely mine, then."

I drove and Mercal navigated. Because of this, we survived long enough to get lost. Our arrival was safe and somewhat eventual. We ate our fish and chips in a shelter on the seafront.

There was a strong breeze blowing and Mercal had to pause to tie back her hair. When we first met she was called Susan Brody and her hair was a beautiful red. After two weeks at drama school, she began to dye it blonde. "No-one wants to fuck a ginger girl, Paul," she'd explained with a wag of her finger.

"What's the boy's name?" I said.

She held up a large chip for examination and then scoffed it. "My son?" she said, chewing and wiping her mouth with her hand.

"Don't be annoying."

"Romeo."

I choked. "Seriously?"

"You're such a cynic," she said, shaking her head.

"Why didn't you tell me about him?"

She shrugged. "None of your business."

"That's true. But not the best excuse from the most indiscreet person in the universe."

"It's not an excuse. I don't make excuses." She screwed her chip papers up into and ball and kicked off her shoes. "Come on, let's paddle."

~~~

I was starring in an advert for sofa beds the next day, so young Romeo was ensconced by the time I got home. I found him at the kitchen table smoking and drinking a glass of red wine. He was a good-looking boy, of course, his red hair stylishly spiked and tousled.

We introduced ourselves and shook hands. "People call me R," he added.

"Very agricultural," I observed with a smile.

Romeo sipped his wine and flicked his ash on to the floor. "Funny, but far from original."

"That's me. Is your mother about?"

The question seemed to exhaust him. "I don't think so. I don't really know. I haven't seen her for a while."

"Fair enough," I said.

He drank some more wine, took a pull on his cigarette and looked out the darkened window.

"I'll leave you to it, then. Help yourself to anything you want."

"I will."

I found Mercal in her bedroom. She was sitting back against the headboard with her knees up, a script on her lap.

"Hello, mummy dearest," I said, taking the chair opposite the bed.

She smiled an aggressive smile. "You're a fool and you have the nerve to be proud of it."

"I have to excel wherever I can. So, how are the two of you getting along?"

"Ecstatically, of course. How could it be otherwise? Is he still about?"

"He's down in the kitchen drinking your wine."

"I'd rather hoped he'd go out," she said, picking gloomily at the varnish on her toenails. "What on earth does one do with the young?"

"Try not to resent them, I suppose."

"Impossible." Her face softened guilefully. "You probably wouldn't," she said giving me the big-eye treatment, "consider doing blokey things with him."

"I probably wouldn't."

"Not even for me?"

~ ~ ~

Romeo settled into the house like an animal marking out its territory. An insidious tidiness and order began to nibble at the edges of the haphazard liberality that had governed Mercal's acquisitions and decor down the years. If she liked a thing she bought it and found a place for it amongst all the other various and sundry and often preposterous items she'd picked up on her travels around the world. And, when it came to her philosophy of interior design, if one bright colour was good, then three bright colours had to be three times better. In every intriguingly overcrowded room, walls and rugs and furnishings did their utmost to upstage each other with a joyous elbowing and jostling. At least, that was my view on it. Romeo apparently had less patience with his mother's careless inclusiveness. Ornaments and paintings began to disappear from the rooms downstairs and bit by bit they were transformed in a manner that was both tasteful and anodyne, particularly when some of Romeo's less exquisite friends arrived with ladders and pots of paint.

Mercal and I had a drink together the night she got back from a month filming in the States. The living room had been transformed into an echoing space, all glass and chrome and black furniture.

"Have you seen Romeo?" I asked.

Mercal sat with inappropriate ease on a chair resembling a piece of industrial machinery, a red

cowboy hat on her raised knee. "He left me a note,"
she said with a yawn.

"So what do you think?"

"About what?"

"The room, the decor, the furniture."

She shifted in the chair with a grunt of pain and a
slight frown and then smiled. "Makes a change."
She jingled the ice in her glass before pressing it to
her forehead.

"Only if you've never been in an airport lounge."

"I think it has a certain clarity of purpose."

"Do you know what's happened to the stuff that's
gone? Some of the artwork must be worth a bob or
two."

"Possibly. Does it matter?"

"Well your son now has a rather flashy car."

"And?"

"You don't think that's suspicious?"

She sighed. "You're beginning to sound like the
detective in that dreary play you toured around the
provinces."

"You don't care?"

"He's my child. He's Mercal Mercali's child. How
would it look if I denied him anything?"

~~~

In the end it was a pirate that sank my sad little
ship. I came home from a location job a few weeks
later and discovered Romeo in my room dressed in
my Bloody Ben outfit, evidence of another one of my
many might-have-beens. Bloody Ben was a small
but laughably well-paid part in an insanely successful buccaneer blockbuster it would now choke me to
name. But poor old Bloody Ben went over the side in
the first script edit. I thought the way I looked hold-

ing my cutlass back at the costume fitting would amuse Mercal, so when they gave me the old heave-ho, I asked if I could take my own little bit of swashbuckle home with me. I knew it would be difficult for the director to say no right after dumping me from the picture before it had even started filming. It made for an interesting evening with Mercal, anyway.

Romeo didn't even have the diplomacy to appear embarrassed. The hat was too small for his large head. Satisfyingly, the shirt and breeches were also a painful fit on him, the white thrust of his wrists and ankles bursting out of the arms and legs in a startled fashion. It wasn't a stylish look.

"What the fuck . . ." I said, as you do, as I did.

"I'm going to a fancy-dress fashion show and Meral said you might have something," he said.

"Fancy-dress? Isn't that a touch uncool?"

He shrugged as if my ignorance was tedious and to be expected. "It's kind of post-modern. You'd need to be there."

"Really? Poor me. Why don't we talk about you being here? Since when has it been okay to go into someone else's room and go through their stuff?"

"I needed a costume for tonight and you weren't around."

"No, you're right, I wasn't. And in future that means you don't come in here. Do you understand? This is my room, my private space. It's not open to you or to anyone not invited by me. Not ever."

Romeo, his face expressionless, said nothing.

I tried again. "Do you understand?"

"So, is it all right if I wear this, then?" he said, holding out his arms and staring down at himself. "Mercal said it would be."

~ ~ ~

I was still angry when Mercal arrived back from a promotional tour of Australia and New Zealand. She was looking tired, but she was in a cheerful mood as usual.

"Open a bottle, darling," she said after we'd got her bags up to her room. "I'm a couple of glasses too sober. I'm never flying again no matter how much money they offer to pay me."

"That's what you say now."

She dropped wearily on to the bed. "Are you caling me a liar?"

"Yes."

"Like all truthful people you have no soul."

I really did do my best to maintain a reasonable amount of dignity and not mention what had happened with Romeo, but when the first bottle had been drained and a second had been opened, I found myself blabbing the whole story and adding as a bonus just what I felt about her son and his attitude.

"I didn't know you were so sensitive, sweetness," she said with an irritating lack of concern.

"And you wouldn't be upset if he came up here and went through your things?"

She laughed and waved away the notion with a wine-mellowed flick of her hand. "Lord, no. He's welcome to dress up in my clothes any time he wants. I'm told a significant minority of the gay men in the world would like to do something of the sort."

"Well I like my privacy."

"How very bourgeois."

"Thanks."

"No problem. But now you're in such a good mood . . ."

"I certainly am not."

"Of course you are, darling. You just don't know

it. Anyway, as I was saying, now you're in such a good mood I've a big, big favour to ask of you. Given what we've been talking about and how super sensitive you appear to be, promise me you'll listen carefully and not get all touchy and answer without proper consideration."

"Fire away, but I'm not promising you anything," I said while refilling our glasses. "I've been down that road before and regretted it."

Her grey eyes appraised me over the rim of her glass. I saw an uncharacteristic hint of hesitation there. This was worrying indeed.

"Come on let me have it," I said.

"Romeo wants your room," she said after another pause.

I laughed in disbelief. "Wants it for what?"

"He wants to do a swap with you. He thinks the attic room will suit him better."

"Does he, now. When did this occur to him?"

"He phoned me yesterday in New York."

"The little bastard," I said with a shake of the head. "Getting back at me for bollocking him the other day, no doubt. What did you say?"

"I said I'd ask you."

"Are you really going to let him get away with this?"

She lay back on the pillows with a sigh. "It's not a question of anyone getting away with anything. This house is as much Romeo's as it is mine. He's my son."

"And I'm just the lodger, I suppose."

"No, you're a dear friend. But I'm not sure I can refuse him."

"But you can refuse me."

She shook her head. "Please. I was hoping for your co-operation." Her voice softened. "Is it really that important which room you have?"

"Do you think that'll be the end of it?"

"Of course, why wouldn't it be?"

"Maybe it's time I was moving on."

"Don't be silly."

We both fell silent. After a while I got up and lay down beside her on the bed. Keeping my eyes fixed on the canopy, I said, "Haven't you ever wondered why I've stayed on here for all these years?"

"Not really. It didn't seem important."

"You didn't care either way?"

"No, not that. I was . . . I am . . . content for you to live in this house for as long as you want."

"It hasn't occurred to you that I might have feelings for you?"

"Possibly. We're great friends, certainly."

"Nothing beyond that?"

"Possibly. I have wondered on occasion. Have you feelings beyond that?"

"Possibly."

"I wouldn't want you to."

"You wouldn't?"

"No."

"Would it be so bad?"

"For you, yes."

"You feel nothing for me?"

"Not like that. I can't."

"You mean you don't want to?"

"No, I mean I can't. It's no longer in my nature."

"I don't believe you. You wouldn't be who you are if it wasn't. I've seen you act. I've felt what you've felt. We all have."

"That's someone else. Someone I used to be."

Not understanding, I laughed. "That's crazy. You've always been who you are."

"No, I used to be Susan Brody. It's Susan Brody

who felt all the things you want me to feel."

"But you *are* Susan Brody."

"No, I'm Mercal Mercali. I'm the person I made."

"And Susan Brody?"

"She's an act. She's my act."

~ ~ ~

I moved out of the house shortly afterwards. I now have my own flat in west London. I have become very close to Jane, the actress who plays my wife in the soap. I like to believe the two of us will get together on a less scripted basis in the near future. Life is straightforward with her in a way it never was when I was living in Hampstead. Mercal has recently taken to calling me late at night from hotel rooms around the world. She sounds just the same. Now that Romeo is making a name for himself in the picture business, she sometimes complains that two divas sharing the same stage makes for bad theatre and an even worse life. "He's become awfully grand," she told me a few nights ago. "I'm beginning to see what you had to put up with." Before she rang off, she asked me if I was happy. I said I was, which is the truth. I don't think I convinced her, however. When she told me she was glad for me, I could hear in her voice she thought I might be pretending. Maybe she's right, maybe I am, but what does it matter as long as you're prepared to believe? If you're prepared to believe in the person you want to be anything is possible.

Bring On the Dancing Girl

Sarah always carried a silver hip flask of scotch in her handbag as a bastion against tragedy. By the time evening arrived, she would be in an agreeably acquiescent mood. A shy greeting and a boyish smile might gain you the gift of a sixpence during the afternoon, linger until you could hear laughter and the clink of crystal on the other side of the living room door and the sixpence became half-a-crown, pure alchemy to an enterprising young lad.

Mother and Sarah were old comrades. They had been chorus girls together back in an era of knowing innocence, before the masquerade of chastity became unfashionable. Sarah had been beautiful then, easy on the eye but not so easy on the pocket. Rich young men charmed and champagned her nightly in the hope of high kicks in the bedroom and the chance of a prurient nudge and a wink later over drinks in their clubs. Sarah permitted herself to fall on occasion, mother hinted, but never too soon or too cheaply.

Later, Sarah became an author, writing a hat-trick of frank yet morally ambiguous novels about beautiful young ladies who managed to be both idealistic and somewhat less scrupulous than they might have been. The affairs in these books were always one-sided and calamitous, the man buying meat by the pound, the girl tarnished and yet optimistically romantic.

This was all in the past by the time Sarah became our sometime house guest. By then she was a theatrically peculiar old lady with a foul mouth and a fondness for gaudy if rather frayed attire. Because her life had been a racetrack of last minute swerves and head-on crashes, she had no home of her own and very little cash and this forced her to survive on the favours of friends. Every winter, she looked after a villa in Antibes on the Riviera. It belonged to Boris, one of her ex-beaus, a compassionate man when compassion cost him nothing and suited his purposes. Sarah habitually came to stay with mother and I in the Spring, her loud laughter, sweet singing, and adventurous piano playing a soundtrack to my growing up. Mother enjoyed her company, but after several chaotic weeks she was usually content to see her leave, if only for a rest and the calm of boredom.

Many of the stories about Sarah have been repeated so frequently in our household they have become as familiar to us as the scratches she left on the furniture. One year she arrived hopping on crutches because of a broken ankle. Apparently she had fallen down the steps to the beach while staying at Boris's villa.

"Boris accused me of being drunk," she said, when we got her safely into a chair. "I wasn't drunk, I was fucking ecstatic, but I didn't tell him that. The man has no art in him, no empathy. Can't for the life of me remember why I gave him a tumble."

On another occasion, mother sat listening while Sarah argued on the telephone with a PhD student who was writing a thesis on her work. They were discussing Leonora, the main character in the last of her novels.

"Of course, Leonora was a victim of a paternalistic economic system," Sarah said, her voice rising with impatience. "But she is also a slut. Yes, a slut. Do you want me to spell it for you? That's it. Yes, slut. Not a helpful word, you say. Well I'm sorry about that. Don't you know any sluts? Have you never been tempted to be one yourself? Oh, you're shocked, are you? Shocked, whoever heard of such nonsense. You should be reading someone else's books, then, young lady. Fine, hang up. Go on. If you don't, I will."

Sarah also loved to experiment creatively in the kitchen. To give a little back in return, as she put it. Which would have been fine if not for her distinctly fictional opinion of her own aptitude as a chef. Her true skill in describing in the choicest of words what she intended to cook for us in no way corresponded with what she actually brought to the table. But she lived with her imagination like a best friend and mother said it would be cruel to come between the two of them. So Sarah had to be humoured in her delusion and mother and I both had to suffer for it, an indulgence that came to an end when the stove caught fire. Sarah, often after disappearing for half an hour and coming back pink-cheeked and girlish, always managed to forget things until they were burnt, but the flames and the fire brigade were a surprise even to her.

Sarah was extremely vain. She would have nothing to do with the idea of growing old. According to mother, the colour of her hair never varied from the unlikely shade of yellow she had adopted in her youth. She also refused to wear glasses. Because of this, as I grew older I would sometimes be called into service to read the newspaper to her in the evening. If the story was particularly gruesome or depressing she would interrupt me through a billow of fag smoke with, "That's more than adequate, darling boy. Too much of the world for both you and I. Move on swiftly, please."

When I was a young boy, Sarah would often come up to my bedroom and tell me stories before I went to sleep. Where she got these stories from I do not know – straight out of her head, it appeared – but there were pirates and master criminals, ferocious animals and brave and courageous heroes enough for any youngster. She would do all the voices, harsh and creepy for the villains, clear and enthusiastic for the heroes, sweet with a hint of self-parody for the ladies in peril. I could see them all as if they were in the room.

Later, when I started at senior school and felt compelled to pretend such stories no longer interested me, she would still tiptoe in and sit on the chair by my bed. Sometimes I would wake and find her there in the dark, her untidy silhouette with its attendant aroma of French perfume, cigarettes and whisky lit by the angle of light from the open door to the hallway. "I like to watch you sleep, darling boy. Such fruitless innocence. Forgive a lonely old woman," she told me once in explanation, although I was comforted to know she was there and never frightened.

If I sat up, restless and not feeling tired, we might talk. I remember one of these conversations in particular. It was so odd and so revealing to me – although back then I did not fully understand all of it.

"You know, you could have been my little boy," she said, interrupting me as I tried to answer one of her endless questions about my friends and the lessons I was learning at school. "I knew your father before your mother met him. Loved him even. He was a worthless item and I was a far better match for the sort of person he was. But I understood what he was thinking and that didn't suit him at all. While your mother was tasty young game, his favourite quarry."

"You knew my father?" I said, almost inaudibly, scared to sound eager, not wanting to invoke the usual abrupt silence following any mention of him in our household.

"Oh yes," said Sarah with a chuckle, "socially, biblically and most of all unfortunately. I warned your mother about him, but she took no notice. And here we all are. Lucky for you your ma turned out to be an excellent business woman."

"If mother loved him he couldn't have been that bad," I said, hoping to make it true.

Sarah smiled. "You think so? Not so bad when he was still around and fascinated by you, perhaps, but no good at all when he was gone. And sooner or later he was always gone."

"Do you know where he is?"

"I think they deported him back to Hungry or wherever it was he came from. No-one ever actually knew. His past history changed depending on who he wanted to impress. But of course the lies were always so amusing. His presence in this country was never what you might call official. We couldn't prove who he was and neither could he."

"Will he come back?"

"Here?" said Sarah, her painted-on eyebrows arched in astonishment at the very notion. "Good heavens no. His sort are far too slippery to return to the scenes of their crimes. I wouldn't be surprised if he hasn't been bumped off by a discarded lover or a cuckolded husband."

I thought about all of this for a moment, trying in vain not to feel let down and somehow affronted by what she had told me. I had never imagined such a father and I resented the cruelty of having to do so now.

"Do I look like him?" I said, hoping to salvage something I could keep, something safe I could hold on to and remember.

Sarah laughed and slapped her knees in delight. It was as though I had lived up to (or, perhaps, down to) some malign expectation she had of me. She switched on the bedside lamp and cupped my chin in her hand and slowly turned my face one way then the other. "You have his grey eyes and fair colouring, but you're much better looking than he ever was or could have been, even in his own estimation."

I found Sarah's eccentricity and individuality hard to deal with during my teenage years. I wanted to fit in. I wanted an unexceptional home life to react against with scorn like every other normal child. The thought of Sarah's flamboyant influence ranging unfettered around the house and all the embarrassments this might cause left me ill at ease. She still came to visit, but I made certain I had studying to do or friends to go out and see. We exchanged the occasional hello and goodbye and, as far as I was concerned, this was how I wanted our relationship to continue. But then Sarah came up to my bedroom one evening when I was up late revising for an exam.

"Hello, darling boy. Your Sarah's come to see you," she said, wafting in through the door and executing a wobbly dance step or two.

I sighed loudly. "I'm rather busy . . ."

"Never mind that," she said, sitting down and waving a dismissive hand, "I'm sure you can catch up some other time. Can't see the point in it, anyway. I never went to university and it never did me damn all harm."

"Really?" I said.

"Don't be cheeky, darling boy. Virtue is your charm."

I grunted and tried to go back to my books.

Sarah crossed her legs and lit a cigarette. "Do the girls like a swot? They never did in my day."

"I wish you wouldn't do that," I said, putting my fist up to my mouth and pretending to clear my throat. "It's bad for me."

She squinted at me through the smoke curling up and drifting my way and tapped her ash into the empty glass next to the water jug on the table by the bed. "I know, I know, it's a loathsome habit, one of several I seem to have gathered to me over the years without even trying. But be a charitable lad and indulge your old aunt. Surely you wouldn't want to see her gasping?"

"You're not my aunt."

"As good as, darling boy, as good as."

I laughed despite myself. "Good?"

"Point taken," Sarah said, laughing and then coughing like an old car. "However," she continued eventually, wiping the tears from her eyes with the back of her hand, "I'm far wiser than any real aunt would be. I can teach you a few facts you won't find out anywhere else."

"Thanks, but I've got more than enough to do as it is," I said, lifting up my school books.

"About life, darling boy. About being a man."

"I'm not a man."

"Aren't you? Do you like girls?"

I hesitated. "They're all right."

Sarah chuckled. "They are indeed. But you must be careful not to let them make a fool of you with all their romantic idiocy. You must be pitiless. You must say whatever it takes to get you what you want. That's what men are for. To rid silly girls of their delusions, make them see the truth."

The last time I saw Sarah was several years later. I was back home from university for a night to collect some things for the flat I was sharing with my girlfriend (later my first wife) Shona. I was up in my room sitting on the bed sorting through some books ready to take everything down in the morning.

I heard Sarah's progress on the stairs before I saw her. Much tragedy had been combated earlier in the evening from the sound of it.

She tottered through the door, grabbing hold of the handle to steady herself as if she were on a ship in a storm. After a pause, she made a dash across the room, her body leaning forward and her arm outstretched. She swore as she stumbled into the bed and then looked hard at it as if it had deliberately stepped in her way.

"Darling boy," she said, collapsing approximately into the chair and then straightening up and brushing the hair from her eyes. "Your poor mother's been telling me all about this young girl you're intending to waste yourself on. Just had to let slip the hounds of commonsense on you before you go heaven knows where and get up to heaven knows what."

Getting trapped by her yet again made me irritable, but seeing the state she was in and hearing what she had to say confirmed I was right to leave home and lead my own life.

"I beg your pardon?" I said.

Sarah laughed so thoroughly she very nearly tumbled off the chair. Rocking perilously from side to side she clapped her hands in delight.

"That's the spirit," she said, putting her hand on my knee. "Don't take any nonsense. Stand your ground. Don't let others tell you what to think. Still, on this occasion you should listen to someone who knows."

"You've never even met Shona."

"Oh I have, darling boy. You're mother showed me a picture of you and the cunning little heifer. The way she's hanging on to your arm and gazing at you with those soft, sleepy eyes spells out the beginning, middle and end to me. Tethered, is the word for what you'll be."

I pushed her hand away. "You're out of your mind."

"She'll let you get her in calf and then she'll turn you out to pasture. You won't get to see that look or get to touch that skinny body of hers until she wants something else from you."

I lost my temper then, of course. How could I not? I lost my temper and told her what I thought of her. She laughed at every single one of the insults I had been saving up.

"True, true, darling boy. All true," she said, rocking back and forth in the chair. "I've not been a good girl and I'm old and tarty and right at this moment I'm just a tiny bit tipsy. Help me up and I'll be happy to leave. Don't forget what I've told you, though."

Reluctantly I held on to her as she swayed to her feet. When I tried to step back she would not let go. "Give your Sarah a peck, darling boy, before she trots obediently off to bed," she said, leaning toward me bleary-eyed with her lips puckered. For an instant it seemed as though she was about to kiss me on the mouth, but she giggled and her lips slid away at the last moment and pressed wetly on my cheek.

I locked the door when she had gone.

That was the last time I saw Sarah. Not long afterwards the BBC successfully adapted one of her novels for television. Following on from this Hollywood made it into a feature film, also something of a triumph. She was rediscovered for a while and with the reward that finally came her way she bought herself a small cottage in the country. Mother visited her there often, but I, as you will have gathered, did not.

When she died, I did not go to her funeral. I was abroad at the time, as I frequently am these days – I'm not certain why but I seem to find staying in one place difficult. But I doubt I would have attended the service even if I had been able to. Mother went along, of course. She said it was a cheerful affair, the few people who remained who had known and loved Sarah recounting their favourite instances of her outrageous behaviour.

I was surprised to be told that Sarah had left me something in her will. I was here visiting with friends in France and mother sent it on to me in a parcel. I unwrapped it not knowing what to expect. It turned out to be a heavy silver photograph frame, decorated with flowers in the art nouveau style.

I have the frame on the desk in front of me now. It contains a picture taken of Sarah in her early twenties. She is sitting with her legs crossed on a sofa covered with silk in an expensively furnished room. Her pose is relaxed and confident. There is a knowing smile on her lips, a secret withheld, a challenge to the camera lens.

She is beautiful.

Memo Home

What do you think of this, Brenda? Thanks to my new friends, I now have company, a dog to look after. He's called Matt and he's a generous soul. On the beach today, he trotted over and dropped a maggoty sheep bone at my feet. Sheep might be sure of foot, but they're also lame of brain and they often slip off the cliffs here in their quest for greener grass. Matt the dog likes to run on ahead and root out all sorts of items: rotting crabs, dead birds like bits of feathery rag, fat-tailed rats with forlorn grins on their faces. I suspect he finds it frustrating that he's inquisitive about the world in a way I'm not. Maybe he hopes I'll be converted by his enthusiasm. Being a good dog he has every right to anticipate more from his master.

We arrived home and my new social worker was sitting, briefcase at the ready, on the wall outside the house. Her name's Lizzie. She's younger and softer-eyed than the last one and she has a much better figure. She noticed your photo in the glass-fronted cabinet and said some very complimentary things about you. She reminds me of your Doctor

McLaughlin at the hospital. She has the same wide, full-lipped mouth, the same frown of concentration as she listens. By her expression, you'd think I was talking in some funny old-fashioned dialect she can't quite understand.

Of course, commenting on your photograph was part of the usual tour of inspection. Making sure I'm not eating cold baked beans out of the can and peeing in my pants. At least this new girl did all she could to be discreet. Which is more than you can say of her predecessors.

"It must be marvellous to be so near the sea," she said, leaning forward to gaze out the window. "I wish I had a view like this." Being old is like being very young, people expect you to be grateful for everything.

"You get used to it after a week or two," I said.

She nodded as if I'd agreed with her and brushed a wrinkle out of the tablecloth. "Yes. What you mustn't do is sit around and brood. Get out and get plenty of fresh air, that's the secret."

Unable to block my ears, I escaped into the kitchen. When you've been in the army you get cynical about the value of pep talks.

She soon came nosing after me. "You're looking a lot better," she said. Her eyes widened along with the rising inflection in her voice.

I'm getting used to these questions in disguise. It didn't seem tactful to mention that she and I had only just met. The professional in her was clearly on good terms with my case notes.

I turned on the tap to fill the kettle and flinched as the water splashed over my hand. It's eight months since the move to the coast, but I'm still taken by surprise by the difference in mains pressure.

"The dog must be company for you."

I took the biscuit barrel down from the shelf and rattled it at her. "I like to have a chocolate digestive with my tea."

Weary with discovery, Matt had flopped down on the carpet following our walk, but he regained his spark when Lizzie and I returned to sit by the fire. He has a special rapport with the indulgent. Soft heart radar, I call it. As usual, he got more than his fair share of the biscuits. Lizzie tried not to look flustered when he jumped up and put his paws on her knees and started to lick the crumbs from her plate.

You don't mind me feeding him," she said.

"Chocolate is bad for dogs."

Her eyes narrowed slightly. "I imagine it is."

Social workers are supposed to listen to what you say without reacting to it, but you can wrong foot them if you're patient. It's become a game with me, getting that reaction. Because the way they try to dress their questions up as conversation is a bloody insult. Do they think I'd keep it a secret if I couldn't cook for myself, if I couldn't make the journey to the post office to draw my pension? Lizzie is a spirited one, though, I'll say that in her favour. She wouldn't let me distract her from her duty. I like her so much I've decided to be nicer to her than I was to the others. I must be getting tired of keeping myself to myself.

I'd never have believed it possible.

"So there's nothing I can do for you?" she said.

"Do for me?"

"To be of assistance. To make your life easier."

"I didn't think life was supposed to be easy. Not as a rule, anyway."

Lizzie tightened her lips. "That's not what I meant

and you know it."

Given the circumstances, I felt obliged to think of something she could do for me. Yet when I explained what it was she wasn't the least bit grateful.

"Sex?" She squawked the word as though she were a pheasant about to take flight. Matt sat up with a flick of his ears. "I'm supposed to sort out your sex life?"

"Well you did ask."

Her face was a picture, Brenda my love – it's a shame you can't see me here doing my best for you, fighting my corner. We used to laugh together, didn't we? I can still hear us. We kept the world in its place.

"Not about that I didn't."

So much for help the aged.

But the more we talked about it the more she became reconciled to the problem.

"Just because I'm not as young as I was it doesn't mean I don't have desires," I told her. "I might be on my own, but I'm not dead yet."

It was a wonderful performance.

The upshot? Lizzie, bless her pragmatic heart, is to introduce me to the local old people's group who get together every Thursday night at the Community Centre.

"At least it'll be company for you," she said. "But I don't want to hear that you've been bothering the ladies. If you make a friend that's all well and good, but don't go forcing yourself on anybody. Understood?"

"Understood."

Oh, you should have been there that first Thursday, Brenda. It wasn't a big gathering, but everyone was pleasant and eager to talk. They even played a lot of the music you and I did our courting to all those years ago, every song with its own glow of memories.

Faith and I took a shine to one another immediately. Because of this, Lizzie gave me a look of warning over her shoulder when she left us together.

I don't think you'd like Faith, I'm sorry to say. She's one of those thin, pale women you always wanted to buy a good meal. She doesn't wear makeup and she ties her long, grey hair in a ponytail. A serious kind of lady. She doesn't laugh like you used to, Brenda, every part of your body, chins, bosoms, stomach, all of a quiver. Although, she isn't one to hesitate. She had me out on the floor and doing the jive before I had a chance to put my hips in first gear.

Do you recall the last time you and I danced together, Brenda? It was when Jennifer's Lucy got married. How we enjoyed ourselves that night. You had too much to drink and fell asleep on the toilet. We had to send Audrey in through the window.

I told Faith how much fun I was having when we took a breather. There were chairs lining the sides of the hall where you could sit and talk and drink tea out of those throw-away cups that make everything taste of plastic.

"You should make the effort more often," she said. "With a bit of time and practice you could be a useful partner."

I tried not to smirk. "You offering me the job, then?"

"We'll see."

If you continue to glare at me like that, Brenda, I'll have to turn your picture to the wall. I have a right to a life of my own, don't I? You're supposed to leave me be. Trust you not to play by the rules, to hang on where you can do no good.

Lizzie was pleased with my progress, anyway. She

had a smile on her lips when she arrived.

"I hear a particular person and you have really hit it off," she said as I showed her in.

"Faith says I have potential."

Her smile widened. "You dance well together."

"My potential doesn't stop there."

"Just remember what I told you," she said, true to form. But she couldn't quite manage the necessary straight face.

"I'm going to have private lessons."

She held up her hand. "I'm not listening."

"With a glass of sherry beforehand to warm us up."

"This dog of yours is no better than a rug," she said, bending to tickle Matt's ears. "He's always asleep. Aren't you, boy? Always asleep."

Poor old Matt. He couldn't tell her he'd exhausted himself earlier snapping at my heels as I waltzed around the room holding my overcoat in my arms. You always said I was a dreamy-headed fool, that I believe what I want to believe. It hurts me to admit it, Brenda, but how right you were.

Everything was fine when I arrived. I had a pair of comfortable shoes in a paper carrier bag in one hand and a bottle of Harvey's Bristol Cream in the other. Faith met me at the door with a smile. If only I'd known.

There was a photograph of Margaret Thatcher on a side table in the living room and no television. You know how suspicious I am of people who don't have a TV. I probably pulled a face as I sat down on the sofa to change my shoes, but luckily Faith's mind was elsewhere.

"Are you ready?" she said, holding out her arms.

I told her I was. More than ready – but I kept that to myself.

Our first few attempts at a routine were tentative, but soon my feet were going where they were supposed to go.

"Superb," puffed Faith as we reversed and kicked back our heels in perfect unison. "It just shows what you can do when you put your mind to it."

Triumphant, I was still in a spin when we paused for our second glass of sherry. Faith sat close to me on the sofa, her knee touching mine. She sipped her drink and dabbed at the drops of perspiration on her brow with a pink tissue. When I asked her what we were going to try next she smiled shyly and told me that I'd have to wait and see. Wait and see? Why, it was as much as I could do not to swig my sherry in a single gulp.

My legs felt quite weak when she took my hand and we stood up. Anticipation sent my thoughts running on ahead. As she drew me after her, my imagination had already scaled the stairs with the vitality of a much younger and fitter man and flung open the bedroom door. What mysteries lay revealed. I saw soft lighting and a bed with black silk sheets. I saw Faith lying naked on it, a string of pearls between her breasts. My poor old heart was beating so hard it hurt in my chest.

The vision switched off with a snap. Faith was saying something to me and the words didn't seem to fit.

"The tango?" I repeated, almost tumbling flat on my face as she stepped nimbly out of my arms and crossed to the CD player.

"The dance of love," she said, swaying her slim hips as the music began, her smile conspiratorial. "There's nothing to it. But you mustn't hold back, you mustn't be timid. Just allow the rhythm to sweep you along." She sighed to herself. "Clifford and I loved to tango out on the terrace of the European Club at dusk. There wasn't an orchestra, just Feydor on the piano, but we didn't mind."

Now, I've never much liked the tango, as you well know, Brenda. But I entered into the spirit of the dance with as much enthusiasm as I could muster. And I have to confess that Faith was a good partner, so good that I got over my disappointment in no time at all. My oh my, the way she threw back her pony-tail in abandon and thrust her bony ribs tightly against me as she aimed us toward the set of Encyclopaedia Britannica on the bookshelf on the far side of the room, was sure to lead to my downfall. I was swept along right enough, but not by the rhythm. I still don't know why I did what I did – my only defence is that it appeared appropriate at the time.

I'm not about to go into detail, Brenda. Much as I can hear you laughing. All I'm prepared to say is that we both ended rolling on the floor and at some point she bit me on the nose.

"Ouch!" I said, pulling away. "What did you do that for?"

"You dirty old devil," she said, panting a little as she rested back against the sofa and straightened her clothes. "You realise what you've done, don't you. Spoilt absolutely everything. Behaving like some sort of wild beast. What next? Good grief. I haven't let a man put his hands on me like that since my poor Clifford passed away. And nor will I. You should be ashamed of yourself at your age. I'd have thought you'd be beyond such things by now."

What could I say? I've never been so embarrassed with Margaret Thatcher looking on in all my life. I could have crawled out underneath the door, I felt so small. It was awful. Terrible. She wouldn't even keep the bottle of sherry I'd brought along. She came hurrying after me as I was going out the front door and thrust it into my hands.

~~~

So that's that. Faith and I are now ex-dancing partners. I'm not proud of myself, despite the fact that it was a straightforward mistake. I mean, you know me, Brenda, I'm not a man to put myself where I'm not wanted.

At least Matt's happy. He prefers me to be at home and closer to him and the can opener.

I'm just grateful Lizzie hasn't found out what happened.

"So you've given up on the dancing, then?" she said the last time she was here.

She was fishing, of course, but I refused to be drawn. "I'd rather not do it anymore and you can't make me."

"But . . ."

"I've made up my mind."

"You could always take up basket-weaving," she said, a malicious glint in her eye. "There's bound to be an evening class."

I reckon I'll have to go back to being nasty to Lizzie, then maybe she'll treat me with more respect.

~~~

Matt and I enjoy our walks along the beach now that the fine weather is here again. The silly dog is forever running off on quests of his own, looking back every now and then and trying to coax me into following him. He can't understand why I stick to the same route every day, why our interests should differ. I want to be near the young women lying in the sun, their bodies stretched out in ragged ranks like casualties cut down by the heat. I love the slow, sleepy way they rub cream on themselves, their studious narcissism. Seeing them, makes me feel there's a little salt and pepper left for me in life. I know it's wrong to stare, but I can't help myself. There are worse things. Much worse. It's not as if it does anyone any mischief. I can admit this to you Brenda because you know exactly who I am. And if you of all people won't forgive me my weaknesses, then who will? Who will ever know me as well as you did? We shared all there was to share. Even now I can't leave you in peace. Why is that? I want to get over having lost you, but there's this untidiness about your going. The freedom I now have is worthless because I no longer have to wish for it. I've lost the bit of me that was you and I want it back. I don't want this. I don't want all of this. You always were a cruel woman, Brenda. Cruel with your kindness and your understanding.

~~~

Mattie found a kiddie's sandal on the sands today. It was made of pink plastic and the strap had snapped in half. It was a poignant article, a fragment of a forgotten day at the seaside. Both the dog and I are old hands now and we knew there would be just the one. Shoes discarded on the beach never come in pairs. No-one knows why.

Some creatures are easily entertained. After sending Matt dodging back and forth with a couple of fake throws, I turned quickly and threw the sandal as far as I could out to sea, the little metal buckle jingling in the air as it spun from my fingers.

Experiments in History

Today the practice of photographic portraiture holds few surprises. But in years gone by this simple undertaking sometimes produced strange results. Take the case of Herbert Radcliffe.

After his marriage in 1932, Radcliffe tried many times to obtain a photograph of himself seated at his desk, pen in hand. Not an excessively ambitious undertaking, you would think. But his every attempt to achieve it came up against the same uncanny problem.

There would be no hint of trouble at the start, the sittings took place without a hitch. Radcliffe would pose alone for the camera, the shutter would click and that would be that. Or so it seemed. However, on each occasion, to the consternation of a succession of photographers, the developed image differed inexplicably from the one originally seen through the view-finder. Because two people peered out of the photographic print. Behind a stiff and overly serious Herbert Radcliffe stood a second fainter yet easily recognisable figure, that of his wife, Sandra, an indulgent smile on her lips.

The story does not end there. More pictures were taken and it soon became clear that neither of the partners in this happy marriage could be captured on film without the other. When Sandra was photographed, a spectral Herbert appeared in the background, his smile benign.

This weird twining continued. Snaps of Sandra's all-female work's outings showed a faded Herbert unembarrassed by the fact that he is the single sober male in a party of thirty tipsy women. As if in answer, a stout and beaming Sandra became the thirteenth man in Herbert's cricket team.

There would be no change in this situation until Herbert died in 1965. After this date, although Herbert remained loyal and still accompanied his wife in photographs, there was a no longer a smile on his face.

~~~

Experiments in History No. 607

Professor Johannes Spangle (1931-1982) ranks as one of the foremost scientists of recent times. A modern day alchemist, a Merlin of the Atomic Age, he is universally acknowledged to be a man with the greatest imaginable passion for the truth. In fact, the plucking of this elusive plum from the pie of knowledge would become his sole quest, one he pursued diligently until the end of his days. "How," he asked himself in his notebook, "is man to know what is Real when he is never free of the confusions of his dreams, his fantasies? Where is he to look for Certainty when time to think also means time to dream? Are unequivocal answers possible when the Present and Actual are continually clouded by the imagination, the What-is-so by the What-is-not-so?"

Professor Spangle contemplated this problem for many months before coming to an important conclusion: if reflection, time to look back, time to look forward, allowed his enemy, fantasy, to infiltrate every area of human perception, it was obvious his concern should be with the present. If he were to create a drug to trap the human mind in the moment, he reasoned, the narrow corridor of the what-is-so, he would then, ipso-facto, be in possession of the very key to reality.

It took many years and many failures before Spangle eventually settled on the formula for the substance now known as Focalzone, the so-called "mind-filter."

Experimenting on himself in secret, Spangle found the drug did indeed give the subject a more defined view of the world. However, his attempts to record the nature of this view were constantly frustrated. Under the influence of Focalzone he would make pages and pages of notes, but checking these notes later revealed only words such as "window, window, window" or "table, table, table" or "pencil, pencil, pencil."

These disappointments led to an increase in Spangle's already obsessive self-experimentation. He found it harder and harder to leave his laboratory, yet he seemed to get less and less done. In a despairing bid to make a breakthrough, he took a massive dose of the drug. Recording this in his notebook, he then sat in wait of the truth.

He was discovered at his desk the next morning by a cleaning lady, who, imagining herself the victim of a prank, only reported her discovery as she was leaving.

The doctor was summoned. He found a very odd corpse indeed. The professor's body had calcified into a transparent stone, a material unique in its geology and as clear and beautiful as it was cold. It seems likely now that Focalzone had been modifying him slowly over the previous weeks and, courtesy of the ultimate dosage, he had become terminally and immovably at one with the moment.

Professor Spangle's self-created statue – thanks to a fortuitous uncertainty in the law and his ex-wife's recognition of her obligations to history – can be observed by appointment in the British Museum's private collection.

~~~

Experiments in History No. 321

It is very unlikely you will have heard of Lampton Paco DeVere (1798-1870) but, nevertheless, he was an artist of some note during his early years on the London social scene. The wistful romanticism of his softly-coloured portraits commanded large prices and he was deemed by the fashionably unconventional to be a dinner guest of great wit and sensitivity.

All of this ended in 1845 when DeVere decided, one dark and hung-over morning, to forsake his life of decorous dissipation and move to the very wildest and bleakest part of the Irish coast. To begin with his friends laughed at him, sensing a joke, a satire on the lot of the poor and country living, but he grew angry and would not be dissuaded.

Even though the peace and solitude he craved

were inevitable in his remote new home, there remained the practical problem of his long-term sustenance. Vegetarianism seemed out of the question. Despite his almost agonizingly sensitive and sympathetic temperament, his unworthy taste for flesh easily overruled his better nature. Forced to examine the question anew, he came to the conclusion the world had made a great aesthetic blunder in its emphasis on beef, veal, mutton, lamb and venison, meats derived from the slaughter of the most beautiful of creatures while the flesh of the ugliest, the pig, was classed by many cultures as "unclean."

It was with these thoughts that DeVere ventured into the wilderness with six pigs and a manual on their rearing and dispatch. He made a promise to himself that he would eat nothing but pork, ham and bacon and in his own way help to preserve the handsomest fauna of the Earth.

This he did for almost a year before things began to go wrong. Living alone but for the company of pigs for this amount of time changed him profoundly. Looking at the animals every day he became aware of their individual features and personalities. "The pig is the most adorable of beasts," he told the police on his capture. "The sweetest of things can be read in their faces if one has but the eyes to see. I could not continue to kill them. And I became so very, very hungry."

The three middle-aged spinsters (Cecilia Fletcher, Madge Brown-Stubbs and Lucinda Barrington) who mysteriously went missing after setting off one afternoon into the Irish countryside on a sketching party were mourned for many years after DeVere's commitment to a mental hospital. He explained to the doctors there that the pigs had listened patiently to his rationale for murdering them before suggesting to him that, given the strength of his argument, he had perhaps not extended the logic of it quite far enough.

~~~

Experiments in History No. 451.

Throughout history many works of art have disappeared without trace. All we are left with now are the contemporary reports of their magnificence. One such missing masterpiece was created by the Spanish sculptor Gregorio Ruiz. Yes, sadly, perhaps the finest piece carved by this 16th century genius has been lost, it seems, forever.

The work existed in the form of two huge wooden doors made for the chapel of San Marco in Ruiz's home city of Gorjea on the east coast of Spain. The commission, which would take over seven years to complete, was awarded to him with some reluctance after much lobbying by his friends, rumours of his radical leanings and riotous behaviour having obstructed any recent Church patronage, leaving him close to destitute. However, any reservations about the artist's religious commitment were on the face of it dispelled when, after a brief period of deliberation, he set to his epic task with a fervour that frightened both his friends and family. Ruiz became obsessed by the work, neglecting all else. His health suffered, as did his wife and children. No-one was allowed to view the carvings. Even the guards that came with the gold for binding the doors were ordered to keep their backs turned at all times while he worked.

When Ruiz was satisfied, finally, that his undertaking was finished, he called on the Church dignitaries charged with approving the work before it was removed to the chapel. Sources tell us the unveiling was followed first by a stunned silence, then a chorus of heated protestations, the artist's conception condemned by the shouting churchmen as both defiant and blasphemous in the extreme.

The subject, spread out across both doors, was The Gates of Heaven. The Pope beamed a welcome from the top left-hand corner, while the King smiled down from the right. Save for their simple peasant shoes they were totally naked, the anatomy of their bodies rendered with the skill of a master. From the waist down they were twisted so that their buttocks were offered in salute to the incoming congregation. Below the Pope and the King, Ruiz's Heavenly realm stretched off into the distance, a world of pain, peopled with a tumble of writhing figures, their features contorted, each face a familiar one, real to the life. Every form of torture was represented and those being ripped and stabbed and burnt in the carving were those in authority in the city, all of whom had opposed or punished Ruiz in one way or another in his struggle to survive as an artist. It was an afterlife of revenge.

Ruiz had discovered self-expression several centuries too early.

The priests were heartily shocked. Many saw their own faces included. They gave orders for the doors to be destroyed and for Ruiz to be taken into custody. On hearing this, the artist fell to the floor, apparently gripped by a seizure, his family and friends crowding around and carrying him off to his home. Whether this was a ploy to save his life cannot be said. All that is known is that later that same day he recovered and, sometime after this, the doors vanished forever.

One source has it that Ruiz called a meeting of all

the artists in the city and that together they helped him to carry The Gates of Heaven to a cliff nearby overlooking the sea. But what really happened that night remains a mystery. According to local legend, a drunken peasant claimed to have seen Ruiz fly from on high as the moon rose, following his masterpieces to destruction. All that is known for sure is that the next morning the artist was washed up on the rocks.

It is said he was still smiling.

Had we not Loved so Kindly

The support band were friends from the old days. Following the gig, McLintock broke a rule and went with them to the pub across the road. The company was good, but after an hour he was ready to say his farewells and get back to the hotel and grab some sleep. He was halfway out of his seat when the girl, Gemma, introduced herself and sat down opposite him.

"I need to talk to you because you're the only one who'll understand," she said.

McLintock looked over her shoulder at the door, imagining with a sigh the feeling as it closed behind him. "What makes you think that?"

She told him. She simply had to get into the business. All her friends told her she could sing and she planned to write her own songs and play the folk clubs, build up a following and eventually get a recording contract. Her parents wouldn't listen, arguing she should stay at college and take her degree before rushing into something with so little chance of success. Her feelings didn't matter to them. Music didn't move them. Nothing moved them. They were like strangers to her now.

"You just threw your guitar in the back of the car and left for good. Didn't even take a second look," she said, her eyes wide. "I read that on Wikipedia. The coolest thing. That's what I want to do."

McLintock knew the story. Knew it all too well. It had been repeated so many times over the years in the press and on TV and radio it had become true. So true, he couldn't deny it without sounding like a liar. Maybe he'd made it up in an interview back at the start, made it up because he wanted to believe in it himself.

It was only now that the leaving was easy.

~~~

Moira and McLintock met at senior school and began going out toward the end of his incarceration there. Moira was a year younger and a lifetime wiser. There was never any doubt in her mind as to who she was and what the future would offer. She knew in detail what she wanted from her life and, fortunately for him, he was on the list. Her certainty amazed him, their days together clearer and brighter for it. To play the guitar and sing and be with her became all he desired. He loved the warm, secure feeling that sheltered them when they were together, no room and no need for anyone else in their world. He rang out like a sour note in his own family, never able to say or do the right thing to please his parents. To them he was a puzzle, a strange child with contrary opinions and a head confused with impractical imaginings. While his three older brothers spoke in a language he didn't want to understand or value, comrades-in-arms in their love of football, drinking and fighting. Moira was his escape, his ticket to some other better place. She alone was as real to him as he was to himself. His life felt uncomplicated for once. It would be her and music.

He left school as soon as he could and moved the few miles to the coast and found digs and got a job working on his uncle's fishing boat. Saved up his pay and bought himself an expensive Gibson guitar and a cheap Ford car. When he wasn't at sea or with Moira, he played the local folk clubs. After some embarrassment and hesitation, he began to do well. Soon he was writing his own songs, eventually making enough of a name for himself to get regular paying gigs in Edinburgh and Glasgow. After a year or so he discovered he'd become a professional musician.

~~~

McLintock got on well with Moira's parents, but she was a clever girl, an only child, with hopes of something better, so they did little to encourage the relationship. Lies had to be told and alibis manufactured with friends if the two of them wanted to get away together. They would drive up and stay the night in McLintock's uncle's caravan further up the east coast. McLintock loved their simple breakfasts, steam on the windows and the smell of coffee brewing and bread toasting. Afterwards, they would take early morning walks along the beach, tears in their eyes from the wind off the sea, the very breath buffeted out of them.

"You rescued me," he told her one time, stopping and holding her tight against his chest and making her look at him.

She laughed. "From what?"

"From nothing," he said, smiling, surprised by his

own words, their accidental truth. "You rescued me from nothing at all."

"That much, eh?"

"Too much. More of it than I could stand."

"Then you owe me," she said, burying her cold face in the up-turned collar of his jacket. "You're all mine and I'll never need to share."

But the debt, such as it was, would never be paid. The more McLintock travelled, the more he was rescued, the less time he had for the person who had set him free.

~ ~ ~

He'd gone down to London in '70 and again in '71. The first time he'd only played floor spots, but the following year he'd managed to secure a couple of paid bookings under his own name. He asked Moira to go with him, then. Showing off, no doubt. All they had with them was a change of clothes and just enough money for petrol, but they didn't care. They stayed with whoever would have them. Made love when they were left alone. The gigs went well and there were offers of more work, there was even talk of a recording contract with a small label. Moira sat at the back of the clubs while he played and read her books, studying for her university entrance and making notes. At the end of a number, she'd look up and smile and clap enthusiastically, but the rest of the time she was distracted.

Afterwards, he'd ask her if he'd been any good.

"You're always good," she'd reply.

When he was approached about making a record, she'd encouraged him, accepting the logic of the idea with a confidence he'd envied.

"But I'll have to move down south," he'd said.

"To make the record, yes."

Nothing more was said and they returned across the border. McLintock worked the folk clubs of the cities and towns of Scotland, but he kept in touch with the record producer down south, putting him off for as long as he could.

~ ~ ~

His home town remained as it was, but he changed, becoming himself, free and unrepentant. Every time he abandoned his gypsy existence to return there, he felt bound around by the life he'd once lived, roped and tied by the memories he wanted to leave behind. He wanted Moira to remain the same, nevertheless, and she did. He came home to her, only to her, but he didn't bring the truth back with him. He didn't tell her about the crowded gigs and the sweat and the noise and the loneliness that followed and had to be chased away. The long nights in small towns when he'd stayed up and smoked and drunk and played and sung too much with the other musicians he'd met and made stoned, animal love to the girls who wanted to possess the person they thought he was for a few minutes or hours and were eager to be used by him.

With Moira time stopped, they did the things they always did, went to the cinema or the pub, drove to the caravan for the weekend, walked, talked, made plans. But now when they made plans, McClintock told lies. Everywhere else his life was running away with him, he couldn't slow it down; he didn't want to slow it down. He told himself he had a choice when he was with Moira, but he knew the decision had already been made.

It was a weekend to remember. The warmer weather meant they could sit outside the caravan in the sun. Moira read, her long, black hair falling around her beautiful, serious face, and McClintock watched her and played the guitar. Nothing much was said. Nothing much needed to be said. They went to the pub on the site at lunchtime and walked along the beach laughing and singing bad songs, the worse the better. In the evening, they drove along to the nearby seaside town and bought two fish suppers. They sat on a bench on the front to eat, looking out across the water as it grew dark and the swags of coloured lights on the pier came on. When they fed each other and kissed, they tasted of salt and vinegar.

McClintock was weightless with happiness. Taking Moira's hand, it occurred to him, with a clarity that would become part of his own secret history, that he might never experience so faultless a moment ever again, that here was a moment to preserve, to not spoil and try and outdo.

"I've got something to tell you," he said, not quite believing he was going to say what he knew he had to say.

Moira's eyes shone with reflected light as she turned to look at him, her slightly parted lips glistening, her expression guiltless as a child's. She waited and then frowned when he didn't go on.

"Yes?" she said.

"I'm sorry . . ." he began.

"Sorry? What have you got to be sorry for?"

"For everything. For what I have to do . . ."

"Do? What are you talking about?"

There was a hint of fear in her voice now. It hurt him to hear it.

"You look so serious," she added, sensing how difficult it was for him to go on.

"I have to go, Moira," he said. "It's time to grow up. I can't stay. You must see that? When you do what I do you have to take every chance you get."

"London, you mean? There's no reason why it should be a problem for us. Not if we care for each other."

McClintock shifted around and took her gently by the shoulders. "I won't be coming back, love. I have to leave this place. It's nowhere. It'll always be nowhere."

"But that doesn't mean you have to leave me." Her voice had begun to break.

"Let's go together, then."

"You know I can't. I have a home, it's where I belong. My parents have done everything for me. I have my exams coming up. I can't let them down."

"Well I don't belong anywhere. And I can't let myself down. You must see that."

She was crying now. "If you really loved me, you'd come back," she said between sobs.

"If you really loved me, you'd come with me," he said, turning away from her and staring out to sea, a cold and powerful resolution taking control of him.

He'd spoken the truth and she'd wounded him just as he'd feared she would and, even worse, maybe even hoped she would. Because he knew he'd wanted to be let off the hook, and this made him angry with her in a way he'd never been angry with anyone else before, his sudden determination both righteous and ruthless. I'm special, he told himself, why can't she see that? I've always been special. If she cares for me at all how can she think of taking this chance away from me?

They did not speak on the journey home. When McClintock pulled up at the end of her road, Moira refused to look at him. She got out without a word and slammed the door with as much force as she could.

McClintock drove home, threw his guitar and a bag into the back of his car and the following morning he drove down to London. He never contacted Moira or heard from her again.

~~~

McClintock's first two albums were only moderately successful, but he gigged regularly at good venues and opened for several big folk stars from the States, building a word-of-mouth name for himself as a live attraction. His voice had always been strong and distinctive, but fans asking for autographs and reviewers in the press began to comment on its soulfulness for the first time. When he wasn't working he practiced the guitar, his playing growing evermore original and technically assured. New songs came frequently to him now for some reason. Good songs. There was a sadness in him, a resonance of guilt and loss that made his melodies sweeter and his lyrics not simply true but memorable. Other singers on the folk scene began to cover his songs and have success with them. The change came with his third album.

He'd been touring steadily all over the British Isles and on one of his trips north of the border he played at a theatre a few miles from his home town. As he drove to the venue, he couldn't help wondering whether Moira would be at the concert. Understanding her as well as he did, he doubted she would.

She'd be too proud, too certain of her anger to acknowledge his achievements in any way. Nevertheless, he knew he very much wanted to see her again, scenes from the past ever more vivid in his thoughts as he began to recognise the places he passed through. He also feared what it might do to him if he did. Fantasies of a reconciliation teased him, but along with them came a feeling of suffocation and powerlessness.

The theatre was boisterous and full that night, the applause when McClintock walked on stage the bounty of the local boy made good. His parents and his eldest brother were in the audience somewhere and they'd wished him well beforehand. He sang the first two songs with his eyes closed, concentrating on his job, wanting to be good, to prove to these people, his people, just who he was, who he'd become, despite them and because of them. During the third number, he'd relaxed and grown confident enough to look out into the auditorium. He saw his family down front and some other folk from his neighbourhood and he greeted them with a nod. Moira was sitting directly in his eye-line in the centre of the third row, next to her and holding her hand was a blond-haired young man wearing glasses. She stared back at McClintock when he smiled, her gaze unwavering and her face expressionless.

She sat and watched him steadily throughout the show. She didn't applaud or betray any sign of emotion or recognition. Her friend, a fan obviously, clapped enthusiastically, his face flushed and happy. But Moira's cool grey eyes challenged McClintock, taking him back to the evening they parted and the feeling of defiance he'd felt at the end of it. She wanted him to look away, to accuse and shame him, but he was determined she wouldn't have her way. He'd sing every song for her, sing them better than he'd ever done before.

He played three encores that evening and he could have played more. The theatre was intimate and warm with the glow of a proud homecoming. Moira's seat was empty when McClintock returned to the stage the first time. Her friend remained, ardent as ever.

McClintock stayed in the room he'd once shared with his brothers that night. It was strange to feel it was his. It had never felt that way before. He lay down on the bed without getting undressed. He was still buzzing from the concert so there was no point in trying to go to sleep. He looked around the room. The walls and paintwork had been redecorated. The bright patchwork of football posters and pin-ups had gone. Above his head, the grainy black and white photo of Bob Dylan, once an icon of faith, no longer watched over him. The strip of pictures Moira and he had taken of themselves pulling faces in the photo-booth at the station had disappeared. He'd cello-taped it to the side of the bedside cabinet so he could see it when he woke in the morning.

He sat up and reached across for one of the two instrument cases next to the bed and took out his old Gibson. Resting his ear on the side of the guitar and holding it close to his chest, he picked a quiet chord, then another, then a third. Soon, not out of nowhere but from some place deep inside him where it might already been written, the notes of a lovely melody found their way under his fingers without a single false step or hesitation. As he played on, completing the tune and then repeating it, he closed his eyes and pictured Moira laughing on the beach and felt again the warmth and rightness of the two of them being together and the ache of moments too perfect, too slippery to last.

The lyrics took him another twenty minutes. It seemed all he had to do was remember them, remember them even though he'd never heard them before.

He called the tune "Nothing At All" and it became the first track on the first side of his third LP. It was a special song for him and it changed everything in his world. Audiences loved it from the start and they soon began to request it at every gig. BBC radio eventually picked up on the buzz and decided to add it to their play-lists even though it was only available on the album. When the record company released it as a single it entered high in the charts and then went right to the top. He went on to sing it on all the TV pop shows and tour Europe and the States on the strength of the success it brought him.

~~~

Forty years later McClintock was still singing it.

~~~

Gemma asked him how he wrote songs. He told her it was hard to explain. He could tell from her frown she didn't believe him.

"If I knew, I'd tell you," he said.

"But you've written so many."

"Yes, and they all came about at different times and in different ways."

"A lot of them are sad."

"But there are many kinds of sad."

"And you have to be true to that?"

"Well you can tell the truth by lying."

She shook her head. "That doesn't make sense."

"No, it doesn't does it."

Success had given him money, a wife, a large house in Putney, followed in time by an ex-wife, less money and a small cottage on the Welsh coast and a life on the road. He'd never married again. There had been other partners, other affairs, other long relationships. None of them had endured, the good ultimately going bad. He told himself it would get better after he became an adult and gave up the one-night-stands and got sober, but he was wrong. There was a borderline of feeling he wanted to cross with each new woman in turn, but there was always a barrier in the way they refused to believe in and he couldn't explain. As each year passed the staying became harder and the leaving became easier.

McLintock was a disappointment to young Gemma. Why wouldn't he be the man she knew him to be, the artist whose voice and guitar she'd listened to over and over again alone in her bedroom? Her frustration with him eventually made her sullen and cheeky. He'd chosen to deny her the answers she'd rehearsed to herself and come to hear from him and she couldn't understand why. Her attention wandered to the conversation at the other end of the table and when he shrugged with a smile and stood up to leave she said goodbye with a cold and evasive look and turned quickly away.

No longer tired, McLintock took a walk around the town before going back to the hotel. It had been raining and the pavements were black and shiny beneath the streetlamps. A noisy group of teenagers stood outside a pizza place laughing and smoking, nowhere else to go. It was town like his home town, a town like all the other towns that made you want to be somewhere else, be someone else.

It was winter and the hotel felt ghostly and abandoned. The lobby and reception were empty. Up in his room, he opened the battered case lying on the bed and took out his vintage Gibson, his first guitar and his favourite still. Throwing off his jacket and sitting down, he began to play and sing softly to himself. He sang all the old songs, all the old songs except for one.

Finally, his eyes started to close and he flopped back on the covers with a long, slow exhalation of breath and slept, the pressure of the guitar warm against his hip.

Us Here Beyond the Light

I am dust and bones in the churchyard now, but I once breathed the sweet air of your world. Lived within these very walls, in fact. Back in what you call history and I call my life, when this house was known as the Heniston Inn and the landlord was old Jacky Collett, famously a corporal in the Queen's army, a veteran of the Crimea. A war largely forgotten in your time, as perhaps all wars should be.

The Heniston was a rackety establishment, a punch in the eye of a place and well regarded as such. Not by my long departed self, you understand. I was the serving girl here and happy enough in my labours until a drunken and amorous farm-worker mistook the innocent smile on my face for one of pride and disdain and cut me deep and fatal with his baling knife and put me where I am, thank you very much.

Oiled by a rum or two, Jacky would often get to preaching the gospel according to Collett of an evening. This was in the parlour, the large, low-beamed room at the front of your house as I am speaking to you. There was sawdust and working men's spittle on the floor back then and the smell of tobacco

179

smoke and sour ale. Old Jacky would sit in his chair by the fire with a full pipe and a grudge and tell the assembled soaks and revellers precisely what a soft time they were having of it, his blue eyes fighting fierce and his face as red as raw beef. Not one of them had ever been as cold as he'd been outside the city of Sevastopol, froze to the kidneys with no proper boots on his feet and nothing warming in his belly. None of them knew what it was like to see a good mate die in the mud and snow and have to step over his body and abandon him where he lay and sally on for fear of joining him. The Heniston was a haven for milksops and layabouts according to Jacky. Damn him if he was not blessing the whole unworthy bunch of them with his generosity, charging their glasses with the heavenly consolation of alcohol, saving more souls in the here and now than the vicar with all his psalms and sermons.

One time a stranger with his face in a pint and an unsteady elbow on the bar was saucy enough to interrupt old Jacky during one of his admonitions of military hardship. Addressing the room with an oath, the stranger declared he would sooner join the army than continue to stand downwind of such boastful imaginings. Jacky jumped out of his chair with a fearsome holler, grabbed down one of the sabres crossed over the ingle nook and opened the stranger's coat and severed his braces with two swipes of its blade, leaving him standing in his drawers with trousers skinned to the ground.

All this ended when Jacky's wife Clara ran off with the drayman and Jacky's mother Violet Mary moved into the inn. Violet Mary was a jovial enough old dear even if she did look like a horse with toothache when her long and lugubrious face was in repose. She marshalled her son to attention and marched

him to and fro that is for sure. No more drinking
and sword fighting for old Jacky. The two of them
would hunch up with a pot of china tea after supper
and play dominos, her pinching snuff from a silver
box and him with his pipe puffing smoke all around
his shoulders like steam train in a tunnel.

Gypsy Jonas would sometimes talk with them
when he brought in rabbits and ducks for the pot.
He was no more a gypsy than the Queen herself and
all her ministers. It was his dark colouring and root-
less nature that gave him his name. He liked the
rowdies in the bar to believe he was a poacher, although Jacky admitted to knowing better. He said
Jonas had a weak chest and was frightened of the
dark and that the game he sold us was traded fair
and square in the county town.

There was talk in the pub of me and Jonas walking out together. Not from me you may be entirely
sure, nor anything like, but from Jacky and his
mother. The notion tickled the pair of them for some
reason. Nothing better to think about in my opinion.
Poor young fellow would get fidgety and stumble
over his words whenever I ventured within a yard or
two of him. Could not have lifted his head and
looked me in the eye if I had wished him happy
birthday and tossed him a sovereign.

After I was took, he wore the silver ring given me
by Violet Mary in his ear. He never married and always said his heart had been broke beyond mend-
ing. Little good this did myself, of course. But he
was welcome to his keepsake.

The intertwined branches of two large and squab-
blesome families dominated the village back when I
was flesh. A goodly portion of them laying siege to
the bar of the Heniston in regular shifts of an evening. The Tappers and the Blackmores they were.

181

Only a blessèd few of us were unaccommodating enough not to share a drop of blood with either tribe or both. Because, despite their differences, they had no choice but to marry their sons and daughters across the unhappy divide that separated them. Sooner this than to some stranger from who knows where. Such as myself.

Even my master Jacky Collett was in a tangle amid this rancorous interbreeding, his mother second cousin to a Tapper who had long ago fled to a village in the next county and thought herself safe.

The charitable spirit who finished me with his blade was also a Tapper. Lionel Tapper, a stupid fellow and stupider still for being angry at his own ignorance if you ask me. I cannot make up my mind whether the fact that my own mother and father were anonymous to the village condemned me in such company or kept me alive longer than I might otherwise have been.

Sarah Blackmore, the matriarch of the two families, certainly commanded her place of honour at the largest table in the snug, the room that is now part of your kitchen. Once widowed and twice married, mother to six sons and six daughters, she was not one to be easily gainsaid or disrespected. Not a big woman but deep of bosom and muscular of arm, her fine, bright-eyed face dark and lined from a lifetime of working in the fields. She took to me nicely enough, or so I thought, called me her Angel whenever I set her glass of cider next to her elbow, her hand with its many rings taking my own and pressing it in a thank you.

One evening she held it fast and said would I consent to sit along with her and have my history told. I looked over to where Jacky was toasting his flanks by the fire and he gave his curt military man's nod and I did as I was bid and pulled up a chair. Sarah took both my hands in hers and shut her eyes and those around the table drew nearer with grunts of approval and eager looks, hungry for what was to come. I was no better than a fine joint of meat crisp for the carving to look at them. The old girl's face was at rest for a moment or two and then it began to twitch and contort. She might have had a fly on the end of her nose she could not swat from the itchiness of her expression. When she started to speak, it was with a growl down in her throat. It was a good story. A blameless maid taken advantage of by the son of a squire, an eloquent young dandy, with a shiny black horse and a rough black heart. She cast out with child from the kitchens of the big house, he returning to his cards and drink without a care. The result of this union, I was born into travail and poverty and laid in a box on the steps of the Foundling's Hospital, an orphan of the parish.

At this, Sarah opened her eyes mistily as if recovering from a swoon. A smile dawned too soon and too proud on her lips as she witnessed the consequence of her imaginings, every face around the table but mine rapt with the melodrama of it, the lot of them save myself gullible with strong drink, tobacco smoke and lack of learning. I took back my hands and said nothing. It was true enough that I was orphaned, but only by a few years, my mother dead of the consumption and my father from hard work on another man's farm. It seemed churlish not to let those around me in the bar have the pleasure of their story, worn out and fairytale though it was. I was not one of them and my true beginnings held no meaning in their lives. Such are the tales we tell.

My room here in your house is now the guest bathroom up on the third floor. A small space with one narrow window, but I had it nice and neat in my day. It is where I was brought when I was at my last, my hand clutched to the wound and wet with blood. The constable had been summoned and old Jacky had taken my murderer into custody with a surfeit of blows, yet righteous ones he felt no doubt. The shadows on the ceiling were what I closed my eyes on, Violet Mary's voice in my ear, begging me not to go. I did not listen.

Jack Middleton and his wife Kathleen, George Conrad, Mable Stead, Herbert Jefferies, David and Laura Fereman and their daughter Madeline, sundry Tappers and Blackmores, here we lie not a hundred yards from where you now eat and sleep, real to yourselves and the world. All those mentioned above, all of us who were once mortal, who were once hearts and minds, bear no witness in your time beyond our names, names chiselled in stone in the shade of the yew trees and the churchyard wall. I only speak to you now courtesy of the writer of this story, who is admittedly both a liar and a thief. We sleep quiet and peaceful in the soil, forgotten to all. We have no message for you other than this: Nothing of us ordinary folk truly remains.